HATE TO LOVE YOU

Lighthouse Lovers
Book 2

SHANNON O'CONNOR

Hate to Love You Playlist

Kiwi - Harry Styles

Burnin' Up - Jonas Brothers

Jealous - Nick Jonas, Tinashe

What I Need (Ft. Kehlani) - Hayley Kiyoko

drive all night - joan

That's My Girl - Russ

Make Up (ft. Ava Max) - Vice, Jason Derulo

Scatterbrain - Emei

Let You Be Right - Meghan Trainor

Light Switch - Charlie Puth

Strip That Down - Liam Payne, Quavo

Slow Hands - Niall Horan

Blow Your Mind (Mwah) - Dua Lipa

PILLOWTALK - ZAYN

bad idea right? - Olivia Rodrigo

Crave - Tove Lo

All Night Longer - Sammy Adams

Pussy is God - King Princess

Steal My Clothes - Kito & Bea Miller

Guess - Charli xcx & Billie Eilish

Your Love Is My Drug - Ke$ha

Bad Things - mgk & Camila Cabello

In MY Head - Jason Derulo

sex - EDEN

Year 3000 - Jonas Brothers

Cherry - FLETCHER & Hayley Kiyoko

ONE

Ryleigh

"I really wish you wouldn't talk so openly about your sex life," Kim says quietly from the other end of the phone.

"It's my lack of sex life that I'm complaining about!" I exclaim. I'm focusing on the car in front of me, but they're moving as slow as my grandmother. And she's been dead ten years.

"I just wish you wouldn't paint such a graphic image." Kim is one of my best and oldest friends, but bless her heart. All I said was that I was in need of a good dick or pussy in my face. I wasn't even picky, either one would do.

"It's not like I said what I really want them to do! I mean, you know I can get more detailed." I laugh.

"Ry," she says in a warning tone.

"Fine," I grumble. That's what I get for calling the kindergarten teacher.

"Did you make it back to Lovers, okay?" she asks, changing the subject. She'd been on the phone with me for most of my drive back. I had been staying at my parents' new house just outside of Lovers, which was good for a few weeks, but they were like teenagers all over again. Walking in on my parents having sex in the middle of the day was more than enough for me to take Alana up on her offer to stay on the Lover's Estate.

"Yeah, it was a quick drive. Pain in the ass getting all my canvases and the easel in the back of my car. But I managed."

"I can't believe Alana's getting married! It's going to be so nice seeing everyone again," Kim gushes.

"It will be, hopefully it helps me figure out my next step. I think I'm over living nomadically," I admit.

"Really?" I know why Kim sounds surprised. I didn't blame her; it was a new revelation for me too.

"Yeah, I just think—"

CRASH!

My head slams forward just enough that my seatbelt holds me back. The belt grips around my neck, and I wince as I steady myself. My foot hits the breaks, but it doesn't stop me from hitting the car in front of me.

"OH, FUCK!" I yell. "Kim, I gotta go!" I don't wait until she speaks, I click the red *end* button and slide my phone in my shorts.

I'm jumping out of my car to see the damage with the driver ahead of me. What a lovely welcome back into town. "I'm so sorry!" I yell to the woman stepping out of her car.

"What the hell is wrong with—" Her voice stops short as she slides up her Ray Bans to the top of her head and stares at me.

"Wrenn?" I'm surprised to see the woman in front of me. I hadn't seen her in almost a year and now she was standing before me with dark purple hair, scowling.

"You fucked up my bumper." She growls. She's avoiding eye contact, pointing at the damage my car did to hers.

"I'm sorry. Look, I will pay to get it towed or fixed or what-ever it needs."

"Great," she says sarcastically. Her dark purple hair is tied back in a tight ponytail, showing off her sharp cheekbones and perfect makeup. She looks beautiful; I wonder if she's headed somewhere important.

"It was a total accident. I was on the phone, and I didn't realize you stopped—"

She holds up a hand. "Save it. Just give me your insurance or whatever and we'll figure this out another time. I'm late for work."

"Of course." I pull out my phone and hand it to her to put in her information. Then I put mine into hers before she snatches it back.

"For what it's worth, I'm really sorry. Hopefully, we can settle this like friends?" I mean, in less than a few hours we'll be roommates.

Her jaw clenches. "We were never friends."

She tosses her hair over her shoulder, slides back into her car, and drives away. I'm standing on the side of the road feeling like a complete idiot. But I know her anger is warranted, given the last time I saw her. Sighing, I hop back into my car. There was minimal damage done to the front of mine, which is good because I can't really afford to pay to have both our cars fixed right now.

Kim's sent me several scared and concerned texts. I call her back and explain the situation to her before I head on my way to my new home.

"I mean, it could be worse. At least it's not some stranger demanding thousands of dollars in repairs."

"Not yet," I grumble. Kim doesn't know the whole story between Wrenn and I. So I don't blame her optimistic opinion.

"Look, it'll work out. I have to go but let me know how everything goes," she says.

When I pull up to the house, it looks different than it did a decade ago. The house is freshly painted a deep blue, the hedges freshly trimmed, and a gate wraps around the place. Not that anyone would be trespassing on the estate. Everyone in town knows who these houses belong to. We used to use it for house parties and spend our weekends wasted and high. I had sex in every room of this house—all during my senior year. I was going for a record: how many rooms could I have sex in without someone catching me? I made it up to eight.

I don't recognize the car in the driveway, but I have a feeling it belongs to my newly engaged best friend, Alana. She has expensive taste, and from the shine on the BMW, I can tell it is new. I grab my bag and knock on the front door, unsure if she's going to answer. But she opens it instantly and throws her arms around me.

"Oh Ryleigh!" Alana exclaims.

"Dude, I saw you like a week ago." I laugh, accepting her hug.

"I'm just so happy to have you girls back in town. It's been so long since we've all been together. It means so much that you're all coming back for my wedding." She smiles.

"We wouldn't miss it for the world." I smile.

"Okay, so my sister is at work, but she should be home later. Obviously, no introductions are needed, but she doesn't exactly know about you yet."

"You didn't tell her I was staying with her?" I twirl around to face a wincing Alana.

"Well, I was going to. But she gives me such a hard time about things. So, I thought it would be fun to just surprise her."

I don't know how to tell her that I think I have a better chance of making friends with the fish in the sea than I do with her sister.

"Come on, Wrenn isn't so bad. She and I are so close now. It's just, she can be a little hot-headed is all."

Don't I know it. I don't have the heart to tell Alana what happened today and how I already ruined my welcome by rear-ending Wrenn on my way into town. I would have to mend fences with Wrenn the old-fashioned way. Through persistence and charm.

"Let me show you around, it's the same basic layout as you remember, but we updated the furniture and style." Alana smiles.

The whole house is huge, but when she shows me my bedroom, I almost kiss her on the mouth. Not that it would be the first time, but I stop myself anyway. I've been living in hostels and rooms that should be considered closets for the last few years, painting my way all over Europe and America. So to see a room with a king-sized bed, floor space, and a closet?! I'm in heaven.

"Holy crap, this room is amazing!" I exclaim.

"It's actually smaller than Wrenn's. But I figured it'll do." Alana shrugs.

I drop my bag on the floor and let her finish showing me around. The place is so big I might need a map to keep up. What I take away from this place is how green and light and open it is. The entire house is covered top to bottom in plants. I can't tell you what kinds they are, but there are green vines hanging throughout the entire place. It's like living in a greenhouse.

"This room is pretty empty, so I figured you could paint in here if you want. It gets nice light in the morning, and it goes to the backyard." Alana shows me an ivory room with green accents. There is minimal furniture, and on the back wall are two glass doors extending to the patio. I can see the pool from here and, beyond that, the ocean.

"It's amazing. I'm not sure how I can ever repay you for this."

"Nonsense. You're like family. Heather and Norah are staying at the other properties anyway, so why can't I have you stay here?" She smiles.

Alana's family is rich, which is something we always knew growing up, but when they bought this property with five summer homes on the coast of Lovers, Maine we realized just how rich they are. Our best friends were using the other properties for the summer, until Alana's wedding. It was cheaper than everyone springing for a room at the local bed and breakfast.

"Well, thank you."

"Let me help you get your stuff all moved in, and then we can crack open a bottle of wine and gossip like old times."

"Sounds perfect."

Alana may be small, but she is mighty. Five feet and pure muscle. She carries the easel for me and places it in the middle of the green room. It looks like it belongs there. I don't bother unpacking my clothes or anything; I can do that anytime. I find Alana in the kitchen, snooping through the cabinets then uncorking a nice bottle of wine. Her parents always had expensive taste, so I'm not surprised it carried over to her. After living on ramen and cheap beer for most of the last year, I could get used to this kind of treatment.

"Did you hear that Tammy and her husband are getting a divorce?" Alana says as she pours me a glass.

"What? Didn't they just get married, like, a month ago?"

"Six weeks. Apparently, she called it quits because she caught him with her mother AND father."

I almost spit out my wine. "What? That's some Jerry Springer-type shit."

"Yup." Alana nods.

"I heard Kelsey and Ryan lost all their money in a pyramid scheme, and now they're back living with his parents."

"No!" Alana clutches her chest. "Remember in high school when we caught Maren's mom with Evie's mom?"

"Oh my goodness, yes. It was all anyone could talk about for weeks."

"I know—"

"Alana?" someone calls out, the voice carrying down the hall as they get closer. "I see your car out front, did you stop by for a —" Wrenn stops short in her own kitchen. A scowl covers her face as she looks at me and then at her sister.

"Hey, what are you doing home from work so early?" Alana looks at her, confused.

"I got hit by some idiot on the way into work, and that put

me in a pretty bad mood, so they sent me home," Wrenn explains. She won't even look at me.

"Damn, did you get their info at least? Were you hurt?"

"I'm fine, and yes, I got their info."

I bring the glass of wine to my lips and sip slowly while they finish their conversation, hoping I can pretend to be invisible for the rest of it.

"Aren't you going to say hello to Ryleigh?" Alana smiles.

"No. What are you both doing here?"

"I'll, uh, give you a minute," I say. Sliding off my chair, I leave my wine glass behind and head for my room.

Before I can shut the door, I hear Wrenn's voice sharply say, "Are you serious? Why can't your friend stay with someone else?!"

TWO

Wrenn

"**S**he *could* stay with someone else, but I didn't think you'd mind. It's a huge house, and you're always working," Alana says, frowning.

"And at times like now when I'm not working?" I cross my arms and stare my sister down.

"Am I missing something? I thought you and Ryleigh got along?" Alana looks at me curiously. I'm not surprised Ryleigh didn't tell her anything. She wanted to keep what happened between us a secret.

"I just don't like someone living here without you even asking me first."

"Well, I did ask mom and dad. But you're right I should've asked you too, I just didn't think you'd mind. It's such a big house." Alana sighs. "I guess I'll see if Heather minds having more company or maybe Norah and Gemma…"

"No! It's fine. I'll deal." I don't want to add stress to Alana. She is already on fumes lately with the wedding coming up. I don't need to make anything more difficult.

"Are you sure?"

"Yeah, it's fine." I shrug.

"Okay. Do you want to join us tonight? We're gonna gossip, drink wine, and watch movies."

"No thanks. I'm gonna change and head out for the night."

Alana nods and takes off to find Ryleigh while I head in the opposite direction to my room. Dropping my keys on the dresser, I head for my closet to change out of my work clothes. Not that I have a uniform or anything, but it is a little more reserved than my usual attire. And I want to show some more skin for where I am going tonight. As if on cue, my phone goes off with the group chat firing off texts. One after the other from my best friends texting about tonight.

Brunette Bitches. The group chat name didn't make sense since I died my hair purple last month, but we hadn't agreed on anything new. So the name stayed.

GIA:

Where are we headed?

RONNIE:

Pls tell me it's somewhere close.

ALYSSA:

We all have a night off?? What r the odds?

GIA:

Not Wrenn :(

ME:

Hold up. I ditched work early- long story but I'm coming out.

ALYSSA:

Didn't you already come out?

ME:

Yes, and your mother was quite happy about that

RONNIE:

YAY Wrenn!

GIA:

Let's focus, where bitches??

ME:

Scissors?

* Gia, Alyssa & Ronnie LOVED your message *

GIA:

I'm pregaming with some blunts rn, so
someone needs to get me.

RONNIE:

Not it!

ME:

Not it!

ALYSSA:

DAMN IT!

ALYSSA:

FINE I'll be the DD.

ME:

Makes sense since you have the DDs.

* Ronnie & Gia LAUGHED at your message *

I put my phone down and look through the closet again. I want something sexy to wear. Scissors is a lesbian bar just outside of Lovers, and I am bound to get laid if I wear the right outfit. It is much better than slumming it at Teddy's, but that is often where we end up if no one feels like driving out of town.

I pull out the perfect two-piece outfit and smile. It hasn't seen the light of day yet, and it is perfect for tonight. It's a black tank top that ties at my breasts, showing off my toned, flat, tan stomach, with a tight black mini skirt that cuts up my left thigh. I'd thrifted it with Gia a few months back but haven't had anywhere to wear it until now. Sliding on my outfit, I tie my dark purple hair into a tight pony and fix my makeup. I already have most of my makeup on, so I just need to add eyeliner to complete my look.

I take a selfie and send it to the group chat for approval. Immediately, praises flow in. This is why they are my besties.

ALYSSA:

DAMN, Wrenn's bringing the heat tonight.

GIA:

Fuck, I didn't know we were going that hard tonight.

RONNIE:

WOWIE 😍

I slip on a pair of sneakers and grab my keys. I don't know what time I'll be home. The last thing I want is to have to bother my new roommate to let me in at three in the morning. Ugh. I hate the fact that she is staying here. I hope my sister is right and I'll barely run into her. I know I shouldn't be so petty, but it is the way she handles everything. Like she thinks I am a child or something. Sure, I'm a few years younger, but that doesn't mean I'm a kid. I groan and decide not to give it another thought, at least for tonight.

Heading out, I pass Alana and Ryleigh sitting in the kitchen. They don't say anything, but I don't miss the way Ryleigh almost chokes on her wine when I step into the room. At least I still have an effect on her. Even if I don't care.

Alyssa's house is just down the road, so I book it through

town and make it in record breaking time. She answers the door in a robe and her toothbrush in hand.

"I don't know how you got ready so quick." She laughs and invites me in.

"I was already basically ready from going to work." I shrug.

Alyssa walks to her bedroom and I plop on her bed. She goes back and forth from the bathroom to her room, brushing her teeth, putting on makeup and curling her hair. I scroll on my phone for a bit until I get bored. Alyssa's room is small. She's lucky to live without a roommate but that comes with a price. I could probably fit her entire apartment into my bedroom. Not that I'd ever say that out loud, but it was an observation.

"Okay, I'm going casual tonight because I'm exhausted, and I have to play DD for your drunk ass."

"I'm sure you'll look cute no matter what." I smile.

Alyssa drops her robe and exposes her black satin panties that show off the curves of her ass. She's wearing a lace bralette, and I blush when she bends over. We've been friends for years, but at one point we almost had a thing. One of those, *we're both gay, do we like each other or are we out of options* things? So I definitely find her hot, but other than that we are incompatible.

"Are you checking out my ass?" She laughs.

"Yup." I nod.

"God, you never change." She throws her robe at me, and I dodge it.

Alyssa finishes getting dressed in her ripped jeans and black crop top. She slips on her sneakers that are similar to mine and lets her dark curls flow down her back.

"Come on, we gotta get the girlies." She blows me a kiss and I pretend to catch it.

Alyssa plays Chappell Roan on the speakers as we drive to pick up Gia and then Ronnie. They both pause before getting in the car to show off their outfits. Ronnie has her gigantic tits out in this cute as hell, white body suit and distressed ripped jean shorts. While Gia is in her usual bohemian vibe outfit, that is a bralette and loose pants that have a matching butterfly design on it. I love how we each have completely different vibes but have still managed to be best friends for the last decade.

Scissors is louder than I expect by the time we get there. But it *is* a Saturday night. Gia's not so secretly taking hits of her weed pen while Ronnie and I are doing shots of vodka. Alyssa is sipping her water and keeping an eye on us.

"Those girls just bought us shots!" Ronnie says excitedly and puts down the four small glasses of vodka.

"Why are there four?" I look at her, confused.

"One…two…three…four…" She counts Alyssa, Gia, herself, and me.

"Y'all can have mine. I don't drink that stuff." Gia pushes her shot toward us. She calls herself *California sober*. She only smokes pot and does the occasional mushroom; it is rare when she has a drink in her hand.

"DD, y'all can have mine too."

"Double shots?" Ronnie looks at me, and we both laugh.

"Let's do it!" I shout, and we clink glasses and toss back the first shot. I wince as the vodka stings my throat but then grab the next and do the same.

Three shots in and I can feel it hitting me. I really should've had some dinner before we came out tonight. I had some fries at work but that was hours ago at this point. I hate that most bar kitchens close at midnight. Like, do you know how many sales you'd get from drunk people ordering food? It's half the reason why Teddy's is open all night.

"Come dance with me!" Ronnie grabs my arm and, although there's no actual dance floor, we both start dancing to the music playing behind the bar. It's an oldie I can't remember the name of, but I seem to know most of the words.

We're only dancing for a few minutes when two women join us. A blonde butch and a flirty redhead dance with each of us. Ronnie and I often hit it off like this. She and I bring the confidence to the dance floor, and the women seemed to flock to it.

The redhead grinds her ass on me and I'm in heaven. She pours some of her drink in my mouth and then kisses me. Her lips taste like whiskey, but I don't give a shit at this point. Everything feels more intense than it ever has. I don't know her name, but her lips are on my neck and the alcohol is definitely in my blood.

"Come to the back with me," she whispers in my ear.

I nod and she takes my hand. We walk through a sea of people until we're in the back near the bathrooms. It wouldn't be the first time I've hooked up with someone in the back of the bar. But when she touches my thigh, I look up in the mirror behind us and all I see is Ryleigh. Like a splash of cold water on my face, I jump away from the woman whose name I still don't know. I blink a few times, and although Ryleigh is gone, she's all I can think about right now.

"What? Do you have a girlfriend or something?" The woman looks at me, confused.

"I-I gotta go!" I shout and take off back in the direction of my friends.

I order a water from the bartender and drink it faster than I should. What the hell was that? Why did I randomly see Ryleigh? And why did it affect me so much? Next thing I know, I'm running out of the bar and throwing up in the street. Which of course hurts more than anything since I've had nothing to eat in hours. I'm tossing my guts when I feel someone holding my hair back. I don't have to look up to know it's one of my friends.

"Come on, let's get you home," Gia says and offers me a shoulder.

I wipe my mouth off and frown. "I'm sorry."

"It's okay. Alyssa went to get Ronnie and we'll go in a minute. Do you still feel sick?" Gia asks softly.

"A little."

"Want a hit? It might help with the nausea." She offers me her pen, but I shake my head. I don't want to have anything else right now.

I know I did the shots, but am I really this drunk? Alyssa and

Ronnie are by our side a few minutes later, and we all pile into Alyssa's car. This time I sit in the back, and Gia takes care of me. By the time we make it back to Alyssa's apartment, I fall asleep on the couch without my top on. All I can think about is Ryleigh and how she manages to ruin everything for me.

THREE

Ryleigh

Since I barely have any belongings, I'm already unpacked. The most important thing I own are my art supplies, which I have set up in the extra room Alana recommended. The lighting is perfect in there, and I can get lots of different paintings done while I am here. Living in Europe for the last few years taught me to live on small amounts of clothes and things. So, although I am happy to have a closet, the biggest thing in it is my suitcase.

I've only been here a few nights, and I have mainly avoided Wrenn. Not that I am avoiding her on purpose or anything. But I haven't seen her around either. She seems to be avoiding me, if I'm being perfectly honest. Not that I blame her. We are at a bit of a standstill, and I know I have to be the bigger person and apologize. If we are going to be roommates for now at least, we can't let the past get between us.

I make a cup of coffee and walk to my art room, as I'll continue to refer to it. It is covered in green plants. There are double-wide glass doors that overlook the pool in the backyard, and I realize someone was in the pool. I put down my mug on the windowsill and narrow my gaze to see a dark purple blob in the water. It must be Wrenn; I mean, who else would it be?

I think about going outside to say hello, but I'm a bit of a chicken. I don't know why she makes me so nervous. That is a lie. I know exactly why she makes me nervous. I'm the idiot who got drunk with her at Norah's wedding and ended up in bed with her. And I'm the bigger idiot who crawled out of bed the next morning without waking her and never spoke to her again. I treated her like a one-night stand I'd never see again despite her being my best friend's little sister. I want to lie and say I was going through a rough patch or something, but I just knew it was easier if I had left. I didn't do long term relationships. I was a one-night stand kind of woman, and Wrenn was young. Probably too young for me. So I had disappeared and ignored her texts until they eventually stopped.

Sighing, I know I need to apologize. It's the right thing to do. So I open the double doors and take a few barefoot steps onto the patio. Wrenn is still swimming around the pool, so I wait by the doors awkwardly for her to stop. The last thing I want is to startle her and have her almost drown or something.

Wrenn swims to the other end of the pool and as she starts to walk out, I realize she's topless. My mouth dries and I freeze, unsure of my next move. I hadn't expected that. She walks toward her towel, shakes her hair out and dries her face. It's then that she looks up and notices me. I wave, will my feet to walk toward her and watch as her face changes to a grimace.

On my walk toward her, I can't help but notice how beautiful she looks. Not that she didn't always, but she somehow looks older than the last time I saw her, more mature. Her long dark hair is dyed a beautiful purple, her dark eyes catch the sunlight just right, and her pale skin is coated with a nice tan. She is makeup-less but donning her small septum piercing. The sun reflects off her breasts, and I realize she must have gotten her nipples pierced too.

"Hey, good morning." I smile.

"Do you need something?" She crosses her arms over her

chest. Not covering her nipples completely, the pinks of her breasts poking out.

I refocus my eye contact and swallow. "I thought maybe we should talk."

"About what?" She drops her arms and puts her hands on her hips. Which of course makes it much harder to focus and maintain eye contact. Have her boobs always been this perky? And shit, why did those piercings make me want to flick them?

"I thought we should clear the air—"

"I'll stop you right there. It's not a big deal."

"You seem to be well…angry with me. Which is expected, considering the way I left—"

"I don't want to talk about this. It's fine." She starts to walk away, her flip flops squeaking like a duck with each step.

"Are you sure? If I'm going to be living here, I don't want any—" She cuts me off again.

"It's a big house. Clearly, we can keep to ourselves."

"Okay." I nod.

Wrenn smirks and then turns back toward the house. She stops to dry off before walking into the house and disappears past my art room. Well, that went as to be expected. I sigh. Now I feel even more stressed than before. At least before we could pretend nothing happened. I opened the can of worms and she lied to my face. Of course she cared, but I guess it wasn't something she was going to admit to me.

I head back inside, following her wet path, and grab my cup of coffee. I set up a new canvas, all the paints I'll need, and then head to the bathroom for a glass of water. I need to de-stress and what better way than to work on something I can sell?

I finish my coffee, stretch my arms over my head, and take a seat at my easel. I close my eyes, pick up my brush, and start on the background. I have no idea where I am going with this piece, but at least I am starting. It has been too long since I've felt inspired. Too many weeks at my parents' house with no space for painting without my mom asking me to put down newspaper or use a coaster for my water cup. They are well meaning, but it is a little bit of a hinderance on my creativity. At least here, I know I can get as messy as I want and clean up when I am done.

"Cheeto! Cheeto!" Wrenn calls throughout the house. She pauses outside the art room doorway. At least now she is wearing a shirt. "Have you seen Cheeto?"

"Like the snack?" I look at her, confused.

"No, she's my cat." She scoffs and takes off without waiting for my response.

I haven't seen a cat since I moved in, but then again, I have been staying in my room as much as possible. Only venturing to the kitchen and bathroom when necessary. I put the paintbrush down and walk the opposite way Wrenn went. I go to check my room, just in case this cat decided to visit its new roommate. Sure enough, I open my door and find a sleeping orange cat on the middle of my made bed.

"Wrenn! Cheeto the cat is in here!" I call out. A few moments later Wrenn arrives with a disappointed look on her face.

"Cheeto! Come on." Wrenn sighs and picks her up.

"It's fine if she wants to stay in here sometimes."

"She knows not to come in here. She must've been curious." Wrenn looks around the room as if she is curious too. "You make your bed in the morning? What are you, a psychopath?"

"What? You don't?"

"It's just going to get unmade when I sleep in it." Wrenn shrugs and takes off again.

I'm beginning to see that my conversations with Wrenn will be quick and short lived. She isn't interested in fixing things with me, she was biding out my time here. I make a mental note to look up open apartments in town later on.

Heading back to my painting, I notice more plants hanging in the hallway. Have they always been there? Was it Wrenn who had this fascination with plants and if so, where was she finding the time to water them all? They all seemed to be well taken care of, but it would surprise me to learn that was her doing.

FOUR

Wrenn

fter finding Cheeto curled up on Ryleigh's bed, I storm off to my room. Tossing the T-shirt I was wearing into the laundry, I decide to head for the shower. Usually, after my morning swim, I am nice and calm. But after running into Ryleigh who was insistent on bringing up the past, I was anything but. It was like she thought I was just sitting around waiting for her to apologize to me. Like it was all I had thought about. Like maybe she was all I had thought about. As fucking if.

Cheeto climbs onto the closed lid of the toilet and sits while I shower. I think she likes how steamy the bathroom gets. Or maybe she likes seeing me naked. Just like Ryleigh.

The only good thing to come from the morning was seeing Ryleigh check me out. I always swim topless and that isn't about to stop just because I have a roommate. But it was comical watching her try to maintain eye contact with me while I was half naked. It probably helped that last time she saw me naked, I didn't have my nipple piercings. I bet if I wanted, she'd even hookup with me again.

Not that I want that. No, I want that as much as I want a yearly Pap smear. I just want her to know I am over what happened between us. I wish I knew a way to show it. Like, if I

23

could make her jealous in some way. Then she'd know I was over her for real.

I scrub my scalp clean with shampoo and groan. I need to be relaxed before I go to work. I need those tips, and the only way I'll get them is if I paint a smile on my face and am a good bartender. I shave my legs, clean up the edges of my Brazilian, and make sure I'm smooth everywhere else. Maybe I just need to get laid. After my failed attempt at Scissors, I haven't had the chance to get laid, and I am definitely due.

That was it! All I had to do was bring someone home and make sure Ryleigh knew about it. Then she'd definitely know I wasn't thinking about her at all.

I finish my shower, wrap an extra fluffy towel around my body, and head to my closet. Cheeto follows me and takes off into the house again. I grab a pair of jeans that show off my ass, a T-shirt for Teddy's, and a matching bra and panty set. Maybe someone will come into Teddy's tonight during my shift and make things easier on me.

GIA:

I hate working with this girl, she's getting on my effin nerves.

ALYSSA:

The hot one? She's totally into you.

GIA:

You're nuts, we hate each other.

RONNIE:

Gia, have lunch break with me later! I'm going on with Poppy at 8:30.

ALYSSA:

Excuse me?!

RONNIE:

Ur working @ Alyssa?

ALYSSA:

No, but I like to be asked 🙄

ME:

I have work until midnight, but I'm getting laid.
Anyone up for drinks after work?

GIA:

Can't tonight, gotta meet Henry.

RONNIE:

Sorry! Opening shift tomorrow.

ALYSSA:

Same!

Sometimes I wished I worked at the supermarket with Alyssa, Ronnie, and Gia, but I barely lasted the summer my parents forced me to work there. I wasn't much of a people person around sober people. I mean, Gia was probably stoned at work right now, and later she was only meeting her dealer, Henry. Still, they seemed to have jokes and things I couldn't be a part of. I was one of three bartenders at Teddy's; one was a few years older than me and the other was in her late 50s. She was the owner's daughter and worked opposite shifts of me so it wasn't like I ever really saw her either.

I grab my work Converse and head for the door. Ryleigh was still probably painting, not that I needed to tell her I was leaving. I grab my keys and hop in. My dad had spoiled me by getting the car I wanted for my twenty-first birthday, so it was a few years old but definitely nicer than some of the cars I saw around here. Work is only fifteen minutes from the house, and I pull into my usual spot at the end of the parking lot. Which my mother would say isn't safe, but I was also self-defense trained so I wasn't worried. Plus, this is Lovers. Nothing ever happened in a place like this.

"Mornin' Anita!" I call into the kitchen. She's been the cook here for longer than I've been alive. Anita lives in town with her wife who works at the Christmas Shoppe.

"Mornin' darling. How are you today?" Anita tips her head at me through the kitchen window.

"Ready to score." I wink. Anita and I have a running tally of how many women have given me their number and a running poll of how married and straight we thought they were.

"Maybe pick someone your age this time?"

"Hey! I go out with one mom and I'm marked for life." I laugh.

After clocking in, I tie the small black apron around my waist. It's rare that it gets so busy that I need to leave behind the bar, but it's better to be safe than sorry. It's seven past four p.m., so the other bartender is already gone for the day. I start checking the bar, making sure nothing needs filling, and then I check the amounts in everyone's cup.

"Wrenn! I need another whiskey," Old Man Blake yells at the end of the bar.

"Coming up, Mr. Blake." I smile and grab a fresh glass.

"What have I told you? Mr. Blake is my father. You gotta keep me young!" He winks and I laugh. He's older than my grandfather with white hair to prove it.

"Of course, Miller." I hand him the whiskey, take his cash, and add it to the register.

Then I start grabbing the oranges from behind the bar to slice up. It is one of the first things to go when the soccer moms came in for their fruity drinks. So, I slice for what feels like hours, and then I check glasses again.

Mr. Blake is gone, but two other regulars have walked in. I grab them their beers and put their cards on file. Not that we couldn't walk the three blocks to find him, not to mention he was with the town sheriff to begin with.

By the middle of my shift, I am starting to lose hope that I'll find anyone tonight. The bar is empty, and the youngest person

I've seen tonight is my dad's age. That is, until Shelly Taylor walks in with her friends. She was my high school girlfriend and someone I'd occasionally hookup with after, too. I don't know why I hadn't thought of her to begin with. Then again, it's been a while since we hooked up. Who knows if Shelly still wants to?

Shelly walks over to the bar in her red cotton dress and matching red sneakers. She leans her ample chest across the bar and smiles at me. Her light eyes catch mine with a wink. Well, that was promising. She's the perfect one to make Ryleigh jealous, and I don't have to worry about her getting attached.

"What can I get you?" I smile and lean on the bar to write her order.

"We're here for her bachelorette party so we need lots of shots and a round of appetizers." She smiles.

I glance over at the table. I know everyone over there, so I know everyone is over twenty-one. It's a lot of our graduating class.

"Coming right up." I smirk and bite my bottom lip.

She blushes, and I know this is going to be easier than I thought. I grab a round of Fireball, per Shelly's request, and place the shots on the table. Then I grab the fries, wings, and mac and cheese bites from Anita and run them to the table. It's technically one of the waitresses' jobs, but it isn't like I'm doing anything anyway.

"Can you get my friend a water?" Shelly grabs my wrist and lets her long fingernails linger on my arm.

"Of course." I nod.

Two minutes later, I return with a round of shots and her friend's water. Someone asks me for something else, and I'm back and forth from the kitchen. Eventually, they decide to start dancing. Not that there is really a dance floor here, but there is a jukebox and enough space. The bride cheers and everyone holds up their glasses before chugging along. I watch as Shelly dances with her friends, but she's keeping an eye on me. Every time I look up, I almost catch her staring at me. So, I wink, letting her know I've caught her.

I'm rinsing off the glasses behind the bar. It's barely ten p.m., and I have another two hours of my shift to go. The next bartender will be coming in soon, and I like to have the bar looking as nice as possible before I go home. I actually like working here, and I don't want to lose my job over something stupid like not cleaning up.

"Are you working all night?" Shelly asks, coming up for a refill.

"Nope. I'm out at midnight." I pause. "Are your friends hanging all night?"

"Nah, the bride is itching to get back to her groom, and everyone else isn't used to late nights." Shelly shrugs. I slide her a refill of her drink, and she takes a slow sip. Her bright red lips leave a stain on the straw.

"You wanna come over later?" I ask.

"I thought you'd never ask." She blows me a kiss and heads back to her friends. Well shit, that was easier than I expected.

The rest of my shift goes by in a blur. By the end of my shift, it's just Shelly waiting for me by the bar when the next bartender comes in. I slip off my apron and say goodnight to Anita, taking Shelly by the hand outside. She's been nursing her Dr. Pepper for the last hour, so she isn't as drunk as her friends. The minute we're outside, I pull her in for a lingering kiss. Her lips are sticky with alcohol and her lipstick. It's not exactly as I remember it, but it has been awhile. Usually, kissing is my favorite thing, but right now I'm just not feeling it. It reminds me of the other night with the woman at Scissors. It's like something is suddenly *off*.

We only kiss for a moment until I get her in the car. I want to get her back to the house. If I remember correctly, Shelly is a screamer, and I want to make sure Ryleigh is around to hear it. Shelly keeps her hands on my thigh as we drive, then the moment we're inside, clothes are being dropped. She remembers the way back to my room, and I don't bother turning on the lights. We're both naked on my bed in a matter of minutes, and I leave the door wide open. I saw Ryleigh's car in the driveway, so she's definitely somewhere in the house. She usually stays away from my room, but her makeshift art studio is nearby, and I have a sneaking suspicion she is in there tonight. It brings me way too much joy to know what she is about to hear. She'll definitely know I'm over her once Shelly starts moaning. It would be impossible to ignore that.

"Let's hear how loud you can be, Shelly." I smirk before diving between her thighs.

FIVE

Ryleigh

A door slams loudly against the doorframe, and I jump, the paintbrush in my hand making an unwanted blue line. Well, fuck. I sigh and grab the paper towel I keep on hand for moments like this. I just need to blot it out and then cover it up with the right color. Was that Wrenn? She didn't usually make such a racket when she was coming in. In fact, it feels like she usually goes out of her way to be quiet. Maybe this was part of her *I'm not mad at you* facade. Which is clearly paper thin.

I fix the line on the painting and look at my phone. It's just after midnight, and I've been sitting at the easel for an easy four hours at this point. I know I need to go to bed, or at least stretch out. I'll be stiff as hell in the morning if I don't. So, I put all my dirty paint brushes in the cup, close all my paints, and then head to the kitchen. There's no sign of Wrenn anywhere, so I clean out my paintbrushes and leave them on the drying rack to collect in the morning.

On my way to my bedroom, I notice a few things on the floor. When I get closer, I inspect them, realizing it's a pair of jeans and a T-shirt in a pile. That's weird. I don't know what to make of that, so I pick them up and put them on the back of the couch.

Wrenn will find them in the morning, I guess. Maybe this is what she did before she had a roommate?

I stop in the bathroom to pee and brush my teeth, wash the paint off my face, and head to my room. Cheeto stops me in the hall, and I bend down to pet her. She's soft and purrs under my touch. I know Wrenn fed her before she went to work so at least she isn't hungry or anything. I decide to leave my bedroom door open tonight in case she wants to climb in my bed again. I flick off my light and slide into my bed as I hear something.

"Ohhhhhh!" It sounds like a loud scream. I pause, sitting up and grabbing my phone. Was that Wrenn? I hear another scream, but it doesn't sound like Wrenn.

"Yess!"

A blush creeps across my cheeks when I realize what's happening.

"Oh Wrenn! Right there!" a woman says loudly, and I freeze. It's incredibly clear now what's happening.

Wrenn and I didn't talk about having guests over. Not that neither of us couldn't, I just didn't know she was seeing some-one. Or hooking up with someone. It's been too long since I'd had sex, and it's been on my mind lately too, but I've been too busy to act on it. I guess Wrenn isn't having the same issue. The woman calls out her name again, and I blush. My cheeks are warm, and I can feel a dull heat growing between my thighs. I should *not* be listening to this.

"Please! Wrenn! Fuck me!" the nameless woman shouts. Is she unaware Wrenn has a roommate? Was I supposed to say something? It didn't sound like something they wanted interrupted.

I put my phone down and lean against my bed. Maybe if I put the covers over my head, I won't hear anything? I try it but it only makes me hot and doesn't cover any of the sound. This can't go on forever, right? I mean, eventually this woman needs to come and then they'll stop. Right?

Only it seems very unlikely by the way she's cheering. Was

Wrenn going for some kind of record? I think about the night we spent together after Norah's wedding. We were all hands and drunken kisses. Our lips never left the other's, and she made me come at least four times that night. We had sex for hours until we fell asleep in each other's arms. I guess it was possible this could last all night.

Thinking more about Wrenn that night and the sounds of the woman chanting her name, I get turned on. Curiously, I slip a hand into my shorts and beneath my panties and gasp when I feel how wet I am. This feels *wrong*. Am I really about to get off to the sound of Wrenn making someone else come?

"Yessss Wrenn! Your tongue feels so good!" the woman cries.

Yes. Apparently, I was.

I grab the vibrator out of my nightstand table and turn it to life. This has to be quick and dirty. God forbid I get caught doing this; I'd actually die. I press the vibrator to my clit and bite on my bottom lip to keep from making a sound. If I can hear them, they can probably hear me.

"Wrenn! Wrenn!"

I close my eyes and imagine Wrenn between my thighs again. Why did she have to be so fucking good with her tongue? I rub fast circles over my clit, but as I feel my orgasm building, the vibration starts to die. No, this could not be happening. I take the vibrator out of my panties and groan quietly. Of course it would die on me. I toss it to the side of my bed and sigh. I guess I'm doing this old school.

"Yes! Yes!"

I kick off my shorts under the sheets, my panties too, and press my thumb to my clit. I slide my two fingers up my wet pussy and start rubbing slow circles on my clit. I need to pick up where I left off. I feel like I'm doing something wrong, but I'm too turned on to care. I can hear whimpers and moans from Wrenn and her *guest* in between the screams. I'm not sure if she's just that oblivious that I can hear, but that's a question for tomorrow.

Tonight, I'm focused on coming. I imagine Wrenn, her soft skin. The image of her in those bikini bottoms pops into my head. God, what I'd do to flick my tongue against those piercings. Her tan skin looked soft, and I wanted to run my tongue all over her. The sounds she makes spurs me on. The circles become harder and faster as I feel my orgasm building.

"Oh Wrenn! I'm so close!" the woman screams.

Same here. I can feel my stomach tightening and my release on the verge. With one last flick of my clit, I hear Wrenn whimper, and the woman screams on her release, a plethora of curses. I see stars and my legs shake so hard I almost fall off the bed. Fuck. That should not have been as good as that was.

Immediately I feel embarrassed, and I look around the room as if there is a hidden camera or something. Thankfully, I don't find one. I wipe off the dead vibrator and shove it back in the drawer until I can get it some new batteries. Then I turn over and toss the covers over me. I squeeze my eyes shut, and even though I hear them going again, I force myself to fall asleep. I need to get some sleep, and I can't listen to this anymore.

In the morning, I wake with the sight of sun in my eyes. My window is open for the air, but the sun is blaring through. I grab my phone and look at what time it is. Ten a.m. Sighing, I decide I need to get up. As I sit up in bed, the memory of last night slams my brain with a headache. Oh fuck. I didn't really get myself off to Wrenn and her guest, did I? My legs are still bare, my panties and shorts on the floor. My cheeks turn a deep red, and I glance at the door, still wide open. Am I going to run into Wrenn and her guest this morning? I don't think I'm ready for something like that. *Ow.* My head is throbbing. I need some Tylenol…that is in the kitchen. *Fuck.*

Bracing myself, I put on my clothes from last night and head cautiously to the kitchen. I don't hear anything, so I started to calm down, until I hear the sound of someone humming in the kitchen. Turning the corner, I see Wrenn in a bikini and a pair of jean shorts standing at the stove.

"Good morning," I offer weakly as I walk to the cabinet. I pour myself a glass of water and grab the Tylenol.

"Good morning, sleep well?" She smiles devilishly, and I can't tell if she's chipper because she just got laid or if she knows something.

"Uh, sure." I shrug.

"Headache?" She glances at the bottle of pills.

"Yeah."

"Sorry if it was too loud last night," she says with a quiet giggle. She *did* know.

"I-I don't know what you mean," I lie, but a blush creeps over my cheeks, giving me away. I turn quickly, hoping she doesn't see.

"I had a *friend* over. She can get a little loud sometimes," Wrenn clarifies. Are we really going to do this?

"No worries," I squeak. Fuck, I need to go back to bed.

"You okay? You look flushed." Wrenn puts down the pan she's cooking with and walks over to me. She presses her hand to my forehead, and I pause, frozen at her touch.

"I-I'm fine." I wasn't normally so thrown off with a woman but fuck if Wrenn didn't make me crazy.

"You feel hot." She smirks, and I suck in a breath.

"Is your friend still here?" I change the subject. Wrenn moves her hand off my head and goes back to flipping her eggs.

"Nope, she wasn't the kind of friend who stays the night. Maybe you know her." *Ouch.* Okay, I probably deserved that one.

"It didn't sound like I did," I retort before I can think clearly about it.

Wrenn's mouth opens for a second, then quickly smiles. "So you did hear us?"

"Maybe." I shrug. It's no big deal, we can be adults about this. But why does it seem like there was something going on between us.

"Hear something you like? Or just something familiar?"

I hesitate. I don't know what to say. I already admitted to hearing them, what was the difference now. At least she doesn't know how well I heard them.

"You might wanna warn me next time she comes over, I'll invest in some noise cancelling headphones."

"Good to know, Princess." I raise a brow at the new nickname, but Wrenn doesn't say anything.

She sits down at the counter to eat and watches me while I grab some milk and cereal for my own breakfast. I can feel her eyes on my back the whole time, watching my every move, which just makes me more anxious. I should've gone back to bed.

"I should get to work," I say quietly.

"I'll be sure to keep it down today." She winks. "Oh, and thanks for moving my clothes. We were in a rush to get started last night."

My cheeks heat when I realize why her clothes were on the floor. She had to have known I heard something and was just testing me. Something about it was getting under my skin more than normal. I don't care that she had someone over, do I? It isn't like Wrenn and I are anything. We had one one-night stand a year ago. I have no right to be jealous over her *friend*. And yet the thought of her *friend* screaming her name for her instead of me screaming it was driving me crazy. I slip into the art room, forcing myself to focus on my work.

Wrenn needs to be the last thing on my mind.

SIX

Wrenn

"Didn't I already get a dress? What am I doing here?" I look at my sister and groan. It's not so much that I minded shopping. Or that I minded being here with her. It's the fact that she invited our mother along and didn't tell me until I was already here, so I couldn't leave.

"Mom wanted to see the dress you picked, and we both needed something for the rehearsal dinner." Alana smiles.

"And this isn't something I could've done online?" I deadpan.

"Please, I know mom's hard on you. But just try for me. *Please.*" She gives her best puppy dog eyes to me, and I sigh. I'm no use when she pulled out the 'ol puppy dog eyes.

"Fine, but if she makes one comment about my hair…"

"I'll change the subject myself." Alana smiles.

"Deal."

It's not that I don't love my mom, I do. But she has a tendency to be super judgmental when it comes to me. My sister walks on water and can do no wrong. My mom seems to forget we are two different people and have two different lives. Instead, she sees my sister as the golden child who made all the right choices, including her fiancé. Meanwhile, I'm the college dropout and bartender, living rent free in their guest house.

"Mom!" Alana announces and I force a smile as I turn to the woman who gave birth to me.

"Alana, and Wrenn. So good to see you both." She hugs us both, but it's more of a pat on the shoulder than a hug. "Really? Purple?" My mother tugs on the ends on my hair and I grit my teeth.

"Mom! The dress Wrenn chose is over here and it looks great, don't you think?" My sister ushers my mother away from me, and I let out a breath.

I follow not too far behind and watch as my mother says something nice about the dress I picked. Of course, that doesn't mean she'll love it on *me*. My mother and Alana get into a conversation about the floral arrangements, and I mentally check out. I walk around the store looking for a Mom-approved rehearsal dinner dress. Of course, there is nothing really my style here. I'm pawing through dresses when my mom comes up behind me.

"Alana went to try on her wedding dress, did you see it yet?"

"Yes, she looks beautiful in it."

"She does. Will is going to be one lucky man." My mom joins me in looking through the dresses.

I nod, hoping my sister comes back before my mom has something to say about my new tattoos or my nose piercing. It was luck of the draw with that lately.

"You will be taking out your face… *jewelry* for the wedding, right?" She scrunches her nose in distaste, like I have a bug or something on my face and not a small piece of metal.

"Uh, no. I'm not," I say firmly.

"Wrenn, honey. It's your sister's wedding. We can do one day without all of this on display." She waves at my face and body, like there's something wrong with the way I look.

"It's how I look. I like how I look, so no I'm not going to alter that for someone else," I say firmly.

My mom sighs, throws up her arms in frustration, and walks away from me. I'm surprised it ended so calmly, but we are in public and she has an image to maintain. Lovers is a small town, and the last thing she wants is to end up on Facebook as the meme mom of the week.

I walk over to the dressing rooms and plop down in one of the chairs. Alana emerges from her dressing room in her wedding dress. The seamstress helps her onto the stand, and I watch as she starts measuring and taking notes. The dress looks amazing except in one spot where it's too tight and another where it's too loose. But we still have two months until the wedding, there's time to fix it.

"I found you a dress." My mom holds up a light pink, long-sleeved dress with ruffles on the bottom. Looking at it makes me want to vomit.

"No fucking way." I shake my head.

"Language," she snaps. "What's wrong with it?"

"What's right with it?" I sigh. "The sleeves, the color, the *ruffles*? I'm not Amish. The wedding is Labor Day weekend, why can't I wear something less hot?"

"I thought maybe you'd like to hide some of your tattoos from your elder family members who might not be so appreciative."

"You mean Grandma? She already told me I look like a harlot so I'm not sure what else she could say." I laugh.

"I just thought you'd want to look nice." She frowns.

"I do, but in something I want to wear. Not something you pick out for me."

My mother sighs and disappears again. My attention is back on Alana, who is frowning at me through the mirror.

"I wish you'd both get along," she says quietly.

"Maybe on your wedding day we'll see a miracle," I joke.

I take out my phone to check the group chat.

GIA:

All I'm saying is we should have more baking
nights instead of bar nights.

ALYSSA:

You only want that because you don't drink…

RONNIE:

I wouldn't mind some "baking."

ME:

Put me down for a big ass blunt.

GIA:

YASSSSS!

ALYSSA:

What's wrong?

ME:

Shopping with A & 😈

* Gia disliked a message *

RONNIE:

Do you need me to call you with a pretend
emergency?

ME:

Nah, with my luck my mom would come with.

"Hey, I'm almost done here. Do you wanna get lunch just the two of us?" Alana whispers to me. I put down my phone and nod at my sister.

She disappears to get re-dressed, and I decide to meet her outside. My mom is somewhere in the store, and I could do without a farewell. Ten minutes later my sister comes out with my mom, laughing about something.

"I'll see you tomorrow, dear. Bye Wrenn," she adds for me.

"Come on, we're going to the Salty Waves," Alana whispers as she grabs my shoulders and leads me to her car.

The Salty Waves is a seafood restaurant in town. It's decked out in fishing nets hanging from the ceiling, and the interior is made to look like the inside of a wooden ship. It's sort of a tourist spot, but it had the best food. So it was a place Alana and I frequented when we went out together.

"I can't believe you're getting married soon." I make a gross face. I couldn't imagine wanting to be with someone for the rest of my life.

"I think I'll be happy when the whole wedding ordeal is over with. It's nice, and I'm glad my friends are back in town, but it's a lot of prep for one day." She sighs.

"Isn't Will helping?"

"Sort of. He means well, but he just doesn't get it." She folds the napkin in her lap. There's something she's not saying.

"Are you guys, like, *okay*?" I whisper the last word.

"Yes! Of course! It's just pre-wedding jitters. Nothing to worry about." Alana smiles and waves me off. I don't want to push her, but it's something I'd have to keep an eye on.

We place our order and Alana changes the subject.

"So, how's living with Ryleigh? I keep meaning to check in with her, but I've been so busy."

"It's fine."

"Fine? That's all I get."

"I'm not sure what you want me to say." I take a sip of my seltzer.

"You gave me such a hard time about her moving in. I thought maybe there was a story there or something."

"Nope. We mainly keep to ourselves." I shrug. It's no big deal, nothing I can mention to Alana anyway. She doesn't need to know I hooked up with one of her best friends.

"If you say so. Everything at work going well?" She pokes at her salad, and I nod.

"Same old, same old."

"I ran into someone who said they saw you with Shelly the other night." She looks at me and waits for a response.

"I'm not getting back together with her if that's what you're thinking. We just had a little fun is all." I shrug. My sister was always a big fan of Shelly, so I'm not surprised she brought it up.

"I'm not pushing, it's just nice to see you guys together again." She smiles.

"We're not…it was just one night."

"OH! I wanted to ask, are you bringing anyone to the wedding?"

"Like a date?" I wince.

"Yes. If so, I need their name for the table card."

"Nah. I forgot to ask anyone, and I doubt any of the girls want to come. No offense."

"It's okay, I just wanted to make sure. Maybe you'll meet someone there."

I nod. But the only thing that pops in my head is the image of Ryleigh in her bridesmaids dress from Norah's wedding. Her green, satin dress being pulling over her head, and how beautiful she looked with it on the hotel room floor. I blush and kick myself for thinking of her like that again. I thought I was over all of that.

"Do you need help making anything?"

"Nope, I think I'm okay. I mainly hired out, and whatever I don't know how to do I've bought off Etsy. Perfect opportunity to support small businesses."

"Gotcha."

We finish our meal with small talk and Alana picks up the bill, which I thank her for profusely. She has a "grown up" job, and I'm saving all my tip money to move out. She drives me back to the house but surprises me by following me to the door.

"Do you have to pee or something?" I raise a brow.

"I thought I'd come in and see Ryleigh." She laughs.

I nod, unlocking the door, and she disappears down the hall. I head to my room and lie in the middle of my bed like a starfish.

I'm tired. Why is napping only for little kids who fight so hard not to take naps? I would kill to get to have time in the middle of my day to take naps. Sighing, I turn over and look at Cheeto. She peeks an eye open at me, and I reach to pet her head. She purrs under my touch, and I relax a bit. She and I get along well because we don't bother each other. I rescued her from behind the bar one night. I had put up signs in case someone lost her, but when no one claimed her, I took her in.

I hear Ryleigh and Alana laugh, and I smirk, knowing how easy it is to hear sound from down the hall. Making Ryleigh squirm about hearing Shelly is starting to die down. There are only so many jokes I can make until it's overkill. But at least I knew I was getting under her skin. She looks more pissed off than I've ever seen her. Even when she tries so hard to hide it.

Thinking of more ways to get under her skin is a little bit immature, I'd admit. But I can't help it. She gets under my skin so easily, and there was nothing I could do about it. I wish she'd just go back to wherever she was the last year and I could pretend like she doesn't exist. But no, she's in my kitchen, my bathroom, my house, and I can't shake her. Alana and Ryleigh laugh again, and I groan into my pillow. Why is it so hard to get over someone I've never even liked in the first place?

SEVEN

Ryleigh

I t's been a week filled with angst and tension in the house since Wrenn brought home her *friend*. I thought things might calm down once time passed, but it seems things aren't changing. I lied my ass off to Alana when she asked how Wrenn and I were getting along. I mean, it isn't like I can tell her the truth. I fucked your sister, she fucked someone else, and I masturbated to it, and now things are awkward. Yeah, I can't imagine that going over well. Plus, I make a point to shut my door every night now just in case. I don't want a repeat of that night.

It's lunch time, and I'm about to make myself something to eat when I notice Wrenn at the counter. She's eating cereal again, and I make a face. Now that I think about it, I haven't seen her eat anything besides eggs and cereal. At any time of day. It isn't like there isn't food in the fridge, but I've never actually seen her cook any of it.

"Why are you staring at me?" she grumbles from her Cheerios.

"Do you know how to make anything besides eggs and cereal?" I ask.

Her jaw locks. I seem to have hit a nerve. "What's it to you?"

"You can't survive off eggs and cereal. Come, on I'll make you some real food."

"What?"

"Dump that cereal and help me make lunch. I'll teach you so you can make it too," I explain.

"I'm fine. I like eggs and cereal," she says defensively.

"So do I, but I know how to make other things too." I start grabbing ingredients from the fridge and place them on the counter.

She looks at me quizzically while I tie up my hair in a pony-tail and wash my hands. Once they're free of paint, I dry them off and wait for her to dump the cereal. Begrudgingly, she dumps it in the garbage disposal and sits back down.

"Now what?"

"Put your hair up and wash your hands. You're not just watching. I'm teaching you—*hands on.*"

"That's what she said." She giggles.

"Come on." I roll my eyes.

"What are we even making?"

"Grilled chicken Cesar wraps."

Wrenn ties her purple hair up, and I notice a few more tattoos on the back of her neck that I'd never seen before. I look away before she catches me eyeing her.

I take the chicken I cooked last night out of the Tupperware and then hand Wrenn the lettuce. "This needs to be cleaned." Our fingers brush as I hand it to her, and I bite my cheek.

"Okay." She takes it from me, washing the lettuce thoroughly.

"I put it on a wrap. Do you want a wrap or bread?" I ask, grabbing the plates and the wraps.

"A wrap is cool."

I hand her one and again our hands brush against each other, a slight touch of our fingertips, and I blush. A chill runs up my spine. I don't know why she affects me like this.

"Okay, Cesar dressing first. Spread it around, place the

chicken cutlet and then lettuce, cheese, and if you like, sun dried tomatoes."

"Sun dried tomatoes?" She makes a disgusted face.

"You have such a childish pallet. Have you ever tried them?" I scoff.

"No…" she mumbles.

"Here." I hand her one and she makes a face as she brings it up to her mouth. She sniffs it first and then licks it. I giggle as she makes a whole experience out of it before putting it in her mouth.

"So?" I prompt.

"Alright, that wasn't *as* bad as I thought it would be." She shrugs. She goes to reach for the parmesan cheese and bumps her hip into mine. I lean on the counter as she catches my waist with her other hand.

"Maybe we should just keep our hands to ourselves!" I declare a little too loudly.

"What if I don't want to?" Wrenn looks me dead in the eye. I gulp and it's like all the moisture in my mouth is suddenly gone.

Before I have a chance to reply, Wrenn grabs her plate. She rolls up her wrap and quickly takes a bite. "Hey, not bad Princess." She winks and disappears into the house.

I let out a deep breath. What the hell was that? Was she just flirting with me? I can't keep track of what is going on with her lately. One minute it seems like she hates me and the next minute it seems like she just wants to fuck me.

We have this undeniable sexual tension between us that just seems to be growing. I would be lying if I said I didn't want to sleep with her again. But I don't want to spend the night with her just to have to sneak out in the morning again. I don't know what I want, but I know it isn't that.

Grabbing my wrap, I head to the art room and take a seat on the couch. I scroll my phone while I eat, hoping to distract myself, to no avail. When I'm done eating, I retreat back to the easel. I'm almost done with this painting, so it isn't as distracting as I would've liked. I decide to start something new instead, hoping to pull my focus. I start with a pencil and a sketch, but nothing is coming out right. I've used my big eraser so much there's a pile on the floor.

I hate how much Wrenn is able to get under my skin. It's like she knows exactly what buttons to push when it comes to me. She could turn me on and piss me off all at the same time. Groaning, I throw the pencil at the canvas and stand up. Maybe I just need to stretch it out, shake whatever it was out of my body. But after doing a variety of stretches, I just feel more riled up.

I pick up my phone and I'm about to dial Kim's number when I remember what day it is. Kim is finally moved back to Lovers, and I can actually just go see her. I don't mind phone calls, but there is a different kind of joy when you can actually see and hold your best friend. It has been too freaking long since we were together. I change out of my painting clothes and rush over to Kim's apartment unannounced. I'm her best friend, I don't need a sealed invitation.

"I'm so glad I didn't need to call you, and I can actually see you in person." I hug my best friend and a weight is lifted off my shoulders.

"I've only been back for three days, so my place is a mess. But please, come on in." Kim laughs.

"I don't care. I'm here to see you."

"I wasn't expecting to find this place. I was lucky to find an apartment, Heather hasn't been able to find anything," she adds.

"I haven't been looking as hard as I should be," I admit.

"You have the rest of the summer." Kim waves it off like it's no big deal.

I look around the place, and while Kim might be on a school teacher's salary, you can't tell. The apartment is huge and spacious. It has a lot of open windows and boxes stacked around her furniture.

"Do you need help unpacking?"

"God, no. I have time before I start school. As long as I'm unpacked by then we're good."

"Got it."

"So, is this impromptu visit just for fun or did you have something to talk about?" She eyes me and I groan. She knows me too well. "Sit down and spill your guts."

She pats the leather couch, and I sink into it. I know Kim's not going to judge me for what I'm about to tell her, but I'm still nervous. I have kept this secret for years now; it was so far buried it felt wrong to talk about it. But I need to talk this out with someone, and Kim is that person. She is *my* person.

"I slept with Wrenn at Norah and Finn's wedding."

Kim's eyes widen. "Wrenn? *Alana's* little sister?"

"Please don't say it like that. Then it makes it seem like I'm a pedophile. She's only four years younger than us."

"How old was she at the wedding then…like twenty-two?" Her face scrunches up and I can tell she's probably doing the math in her head.

"I believe so." I groan.

"Okay, so you slept with her almost two years ago. Why tell me now? Because you guys are living together?" She looks at me with wrinkled brows.

"Well, I sort of snuck out the morning after. And ignored some texts from her after that." I wince.

"Ryleigh! You ghosted someone you knew you'd see again?"

"In theory, it wasn't my smartest move. But yes." I bow my head in shame.

"Okay, so you ghosted her. And I'm assuming it's awkward now that you're living with her."

"Well, no." I pause. "At first, she was just avoiding me. But lately she's flirty, and I can't get a good read on what exactly she wants from me."

"What do you mean?"

"Well, for one, she brought home some woman and fucked her loud enough for me to hear and then teased me about it for days. But then today she and I were cooking together, and I told her to keep her hands to herself and she was all *'what if I don't want to'* but like…flirty?"

"Ah, so you don't know what to do because you want to sleep with her again?"

"No! I mean. I don't know."

"Wait, she had sex with someone with the intent of you hearing?" Kim backtracks.

"I'm not sure, but it sure seems like it."

"Hmm."

"What?"

"Have you considered she's trying to get back at you for ghosting?"

"W-what?"

"I mean it just seems like she's trying to get a rise out of you because of you ghosting her. She could totally be genuine, but if you're seeing all this, to me it sounds like payback."

"Holy shit, I hadn't even considered that." Wrenn wouldn't do that, would she? I think back to the last few weeks of living with her. She's been so hot and cold with me, but now is was hot all the time. It's like she is actively trying to get a rise out of me.

"You could probably call her out on it, and she'd stop." Kim shrugs.

"Or… I could play her at her own game." I start to think of all kinds of things I could do to get back at her.

"You're going to flirt with her to get a rise out of her?"

"Why not? Either she sees what I'm doing and stops or…"

"Or you guys end up sleeping together again?" Kim guesses.

"Well, yeah." I shrug.

"Do you think that's the best idea considering how close Alana's wedding is?"

"Probably not." I admit.

"But you're gonna do it anyway?" She sighs. Sometimes she is like the mom of the group, reminding us what right and wrong was.

"I won't ghost her this time, I promise."

"Just be sure you know what you're doing." She frowns.

"I will."

I think about Wrenn—of course she is playing me. I don't know why that hasn't crossed my mind. Maybe not originally, but with the topless swimming and the constant touching? It's so obvious now. But two can play at that game. I'm just as good at flirting, if not better than she is. If she wants to skate the line of flirting to get a rise out of me then game on. She has no idea what is coming to her. I'm about to make her regret she ever tried to get a rise out of me.

EIGHT

Wrenn

"What do you think about an end of summer vacation?" Ronnie asks.

"Don't we need money for that?" I laugh. Gia passes me her weed pen, and I take a small hit.

"Facts." Gia laughs.

"I'm just so sick of this small town." Ronnie groans and falls backward into my bed.

"I second that." Gia nods.

"I can probably swing like, a weekend away, but only if we all split it."

"I'm sure Alyssa will be on board." Ronnie smiles. She was the only one of us who had work today.

"Is your roommate around?" Gia asks.

"You mean Ryleigh?" I roll my eyes. "No, I think she's out with my sister."

"Whoa, what's going on there?" Ronnie sits back up.

"She just gets under my skin," I grumble. Gia offers her pen again, but I pass. I've had enough hits. I don't have a big tolerance like she does.

"What did she do?" Ronnie asks.

"She's just, ugh… she's always around, and it's not like I can have a problem with her because she's my *sister's* best friend. But she's always in my space, and she tries to be friends with me even though I've made it so clear I want nothing to do with her."

"Whoa." Gia opens her eyes. Well, as much as she can while they're red and relaxed.

"What?"

"You just... seem annoyed with her a lot lately. But it also comes across like you might like her?" Gia says quietly.

"What?!" I gasp.

"Yeah, that's so true. You talk about her, like, all the time," Ronnie adds.

"I do not," I mumble.

"Oh my gosh, she does! It's like, all she complains about," Gia adds, ignoring me.

"She is hot. Why don't you guys just fuck out the tension or something?" Ronnie jokes.

I freeze. I've never told them about Norah's wedding, I didn't want to admit that someone had ghosted me. Especially someone we all knew and would run into from time to time. Do I really talk about her that much? I thought it was a normal amount, considering how much she got under my skin. I've recently spent more time trying to get under *her* skin, and it's working better than I expected. I mean, she seems like she's falling for me. But I can't exactly tell them about that.

"Look, we love you, and if you like her, you should go for it."

"I don't like her! I just wish she'd stop trying to be friends with me. It's annoying. That's all." I huff.

"Okay." Gia and Ronnie exchange a glance but at least they change the subject.

"Did you want to go out tonight?" Ronnie asks.

"Nah, I actually don't. I haven't been out since last time, and I still have the memory of almost throwing up on that hot girl." I wince.

"Fair." Gia nods.

"I have to go to work in the morning so it's probably best I don't either. I've just been looking for something to do."

"You seem to be anxious to get out of town today," I notice.

"I just wish I could do *more*." Ronnie frowns.

"What's your bestie Knox up to today?" I tease. Ronnie and Knox have been best friends throughout high school. He's one of the few openly gay males in Lovers.

"Ooo! Maybe he'll hang out!" Ronnie gets to typing away on her phone.

"Is that girl at work still bothering you?" I ask Gia.

"God yes. She's seriously the fucking worst." She groans.

"Do you work with her?"

"We are both assistant managers in the bakery department. And right now, our boss is about to leave for another store so we're both vying for the job."

"They'd be crazy not to give it to you," I reassure her. Gia is crazy talented when it comes to her cake decorating skills.

"Okay, so Knox wants to go out. Which means we gotta go," Ronnie says, standing.

"What? Both of you?"

"She's my ride." Gia shrugs.

"Damn." I groan.

"See you later, babe." They both wave and I pout on my bed. What am I supposed to do for the rest of the night?

I'm about to climb back into bed at a measly eight p.m. when I hear Ryleigh's car. The gravel under her tires is louder by my window. Sitting up in bed, an idea hits me. We are both home alone; what if I try seducing her? She'd never anticipate it and it would give me something to do. But how am I going to keep her attention on me? Suddenly, an idea hits me and I race to my dresser to pull out my smallest bikini bottoms. I snag the black pair that barely covers my pussy that I tan in when I'm home alone. It leaves almost no tan line—*perfect*.

I grab a bottle of sunscreen and head to the living room. Just as she comes in, I bend over and lather my legs with the sunscreen. Out of the corner of my eye, the door opens, and she stops, stunned in place.

I flip back to normal. "Hi." I smile. I haven't bothered to put on the top of my suit.

"G-Going for a swim?" she chokes out. She looks like all the blood in her body has gone to her cheeks. It is way too easy to mess with her.

"I'm going for a night swim. You should join me."

"Me?" Ryleigh looks too stunned to speak.

"Sure. Do you think you can get my back first?" I hold out the sunscreen bottle, and she clenches her jaw with a nod.

I pull my long purple curls off my back and hold them to the side. Ryleigh walks over and squirts some into her hands and gives me the bottle. Her hands are cool when she touches my back. She makes a point to get my shoulders too.

"Isn't it a little late to be putting on sunscreen?"

"The sun isn't down yet, you can never be too careful," I lie. Of course, it is too late, but I want her hands on me. It's all part of my seduction.

"Uh huh." She nods. Her hands drop from my back, and I turn around.

"So? Joining me?"

"Umm… sure," she decides. I try to hide my smirk.

"I'll meet you outside," I say, giving her a chance to check out my ass again.

I can feel her eyes on me while I walk. When I step outside, I am grateful it isn't too cool yet. Not that it matters; the pool is heated. I sit on the edge of the pool, deciding to give myself the best chances for Ryleigh to check out my chest. I let my hair fall behind me and jut out my chest.

"Can you help me with this?" Ryleigh asks, holding a bikini top to her chest. She's holding the string to tie the top in her hand.

"Sure." I stand up, letting Ryleigh walk to me. I'm about to tie it up when I get a better idea. I grab the strings and in one swoop I toss the top into the pool.

"What are you doing?!" She squeals. She lets go of her chest and yells at me. I can't help but smirk and take a peek at the twins.

"I thought you'd wanna join me." I shrug and sit back down.

Ryleigh laughs as she pushes me into the pool. My whole body goes under the water, and I swim to the top.

"You bitch!" I yell and wave my arms to splash her. While she's sitting down, I grab her hand and pull her in just as quick.

It turns into a splash fight of epic proportions. There's water going everywhere as we swing our arms to push water at the other. It's incredibly ungraceful. We're both in a fit of giggles as we splash the other like kids. We take turns swimming around the pool, trying to miss being splashed. At one point I'm about to swing my arms, but hers meets mine. I swim closer, and she grabs my wrist. It feels like something is about to happen, so I swim away. I'm not ready for anything like that to happen. I just have to make her want it. We splash until she finally calls out a truce, and we sit on the edge of the pool again.

"How was seeing my sister?" I ask breaking the silence.

"Good, I saw the other girls too," she says, making me remember how many times growing up it was my sister and "the girls." A closed-door and close-knit group. One that I wasn't allowed in until very recently.

"Ah."

"You always make that face when Alana mentions the girls." She must've noticed my face.

"I just remember how it was growing up." I shrug. Sometimes it still stung.

"I'm sorry." She frowns.

"It's just how it was." I want to change the subject. I don't like this conversation.

"What did you do today?" she asks.

"I had the early shift at work for a change and then my friends came over."

"Your *loud* friend?" she teases.

"No, not tonight." I smirk.

"Whatever will you do then?" She slides into the pool and then looks up at me with fluttering eyes. Is she flirting with me right now?

Plus, now that she isn't right next to me, I can see her full and perky breasts. They sit just a bit above the water as she stands in the shallow end. Her pink nipples are hard and pointing right at me. God, what I'd do to have those in my mouth. I clench my thighs together, thinking about Ryleigh and me together.

"What if we go skinny dipping?" I ask mischievously.

"Aren't we already?"

"Well, not all of us." I glance down.

"L-Like totally naked?" She's nervous again. Good, this is where I want her.

"Why not?" I stand up and make a show of bending over, tossing my teeny bottoms to the chairs behind me. I give her a look like, *your turn.*

Surprisingly, Ryleigh matches my look with one of her own as she climbs out of the pool. She takes a quick breath before dropping her modest bathing suit bottoms. I maintain eye contact with her, and I lean in closer to her. I can smell the chlorine dripping off both of us. She leans in and I jump into the pool. I make a splash, and she jumps in after me. I'm keeping her on the edge of wanting me and wanting more.

"I've never been skinny dipping before," Ryleigh admits.

"What? Why not?"

"The girls were never adventurous for it." She shrugs.

"Maybe you should stick with me from now on." I smirk.

Ryleigh bites down on her bottom lip, and I start to wonder what she'd sound like if I was the one doing that. Must she have such kissable-looking lips? God, all I want to do is kiss her. But I need to stay strong. This is all about me leading her on but not actually following through. I can't go down that road again. But fuck, her lips are right there. She catches me looking at her lips, so I splash her again. But this time, I run toward the house.

I stop by the doors to look back one last time. Ryleigh stares after me with a confused look on her face. So I blow her a kiss and run inside, all the way to my bathroom. I really need a cold shower after that. Just looking at how beautiful Ryleigh is was enough to turn me on it seems. It didn't help that the night with Shelly was more giving than receiving. Not that she didn't offer, but I only wanted Ryleigh hearing my name being screamed.

NINE

Ryleigh

Wrenn leaves me *wet*. I grab my bathing suit top from the bottom of the deep end, then I find my bottoms on the side. Quickly, I rush inside. It isn't like Wrenn has neighbors, but just in case we have a surprise visit from someone. I don't want to explain why I am naked.

I thought Wrenn was about to kiss me. Just to test Kim's theory about Wrenn faking it, I had gotten closer when she did. I met every flirt with one of my own. And if tonight was any indication, she is definitely trying to get back at me. I mean, why would she run inside instead of kissing me? I stop before going to my room, to listen out to what Wrenn's up to and I hear her shower running.

Following suit, I head to the guest bath and start a shower. I want to paint before bed, but I don't want to smell like chlorine while I do. I am suddenly buzzing with ideas, and I am dying to get back to my easel. Or maybe I'll do some digital art tonight. I haven't updated my online shop since I got home. I could use a few new designs. I quickly wash off and grab my iPad off my desk. I dress in pajamas, a cardigan, and fuzzy socks. Then I walk to the backyard, take a seat on one of the dry chairs, and start drawing.

I wasn't planning it, but I start going for a pool themed design. I draw the outline of a woman and paint her in the colors of the lesbian flag. It's only when I'm done that I realize she looks too much like Wrenn. The shape of her nose, her eyes, fuck, even her boobs were similar. I decide to scrap this one and start fresh. I move to a new page and start drawing. This time when I check the sketch, it's just a normal woman. No resemblance here. I add some summer things to her: a pair of sunglasses and one of those floppy beach hats. She'd look cool on a sticker.

The online shop was something I started when I was away, a way to create some income while not having to do much. Most of it is digital designs, but the moment I have a painting listed it is gone almost instantly. I get requests for customs too, which I mainly turn down, but every now and again I take a few on to keep money in the bank. It kept me afloat while I was in Europe, and it helps while I'm saving up now for an apartment.

I sketch and draw for a while until I realize it's after three a.m. I should probably get some sleep before the sun comes up. So, I close up my iPad and head back inside. I head for my room, slide into bed, and try to relax. I'm tired, but it's that kind of tired where I am still too awake to sleep. So I scroll on tiktok for a bit until I pass out with my phone in my hand.

In the morning, I wake up with a hot phone in my hand and I groan. It will take forever for it to cool down enough so I can charge it. That's what I get for falling asleep watching Tik Toks. I move out of bed and see Cheeto sleeping on the floor in my closet. I bend down to pet her, and she purrs at me lightly. Wrenn must be at work already. Cheeto has a tendency to only come in here when Wrenn isn't around.

I look at the time on the clock and realize it is almost time for me to meet the girls for lunch. We are meeting at the Salty Wave because it has food that everyone can enjoy. It is complicated keeping up with who is vegan or not having dairy or gluten right now. Plus, it has the best seafood, especially during the summer when it is nice and fresh. I can practically taste the lobster roll as my stomach starts growling.

I get dressed quickly, pull on a green sundress, and pull my hair back with a silk hair tie. I make sure that Wrenn left out food for Cheeto and refill her water bowl. She usually doesn't drink it, but I like to make sure she has some anyway. Thankfully, I remember to pick up Heather on the way or I'd never hear the end of it. She is living on the estate in one of the other houses, so it isn't like I had to drive far.

"I thought you forgot about me." My pink-haired friend smiles as she gets in. I've seen her a few times already this summer.

"I almost did," I admit. "I was running late, but thank god I remembered." I laugh.

"I was about to drive myself," Heather says.

"Nonsense. I'm glad to get you. How are you?"

"Good, I'm looking forward to this lunch. I love eating at the Salty Wave."

"Me too. I haven't since I've been back."

"I think I've been twice already. Their vegan meals taste too good to resist." She groans.

I nod as we pull in the parking lot. We are a few minutes late, so I'm not surprised to find Alana, Kim, and Norah waiting by the front doors.

"Look who finally showed up." Alana rolls her eyes.

"I almost forgot to get Heather, so blame me." I put up my hands.

"I'm starving." Norah groans.

We exchange hugs and follow the girls in to get a table. It's a Saturday in Lovers, so it is busier than normal. But we get a booth in the back, away from most of the other people. The last thing I want is to run into someone I know from high school in here. Once we order, Alana claps her hands together and starts updating us on the wedding. There is very little she actually wants us to do. She insisted on taking care of most of it on her own. But we were able to take care of the bachelorette party, which I took over since my friends had more *vanilla* ideas than I was expecting. Our best friend was only getting married once, I figured we should go all out.

"Everyone knows when to pick up their dresses right?" Alana asks.

"Yes," we all say together.

"Perfect, happy to get that stuff out of the way. Now what's new?" She sips on her alcoholic cider.

"I'm all moved into my new place," Kim announces with a smile.

"I can't wait to see the place." Alana smiles.

"It's bigger than I expected, so I can definitely host a girls' night," Kim says proudly.

"Did you find dates to the wedding yet?" Alana asks. The question could be for any of us, but I know it's directed at me and Heather. Kim just got out of something long term and Norah's husband passed away not too long ago.

"Nope." I shake my head. The only person that crosses my mind is Wrenn. But I can't exactly say that right now. It's not like Wrenn would be my date anyway. She and I are just in this flirting standstill.

"I might have." Heather chews on her bottom lip nervously.

"Um, details!" I squeal.

"She's a tour guide at the Lighthouse. We started seeing each other this summer but it feels pretty serious." She smiles.

"That's awesome, just down to you Ry," Alana teases. I know she doesn't care if I come alone, she just wants me to meet someone. It just feels like more pressure than she realizes.

Our food comes and interrupts the conversation for a bit. We're all quiet while we dig into our meals. I notice Norah isn't really eating, she's more pushing the pasta she got all around her plate. Maybe she didn't like her meal? I don't want to bring attention to it, but she's just sipping her ginger ale. Maybe she's getting over a stomach virus or something?

"Norah, how are you getting along with Gemma?" Alana asks.

"Who's Gemma?" I ask.

"She's my college roommate, she's staying at the other house with Norah," Alana explains. Oh right, I did know that.

"She's great. I can see why you like her." Norah smiles. There's a hint of a blush on her cheeks. If I didn't know any better, I'd think Norah had a crush. But she is straight, just like Alana.

"Is she in the wedding?" Kim asks.

"She's the maid of honor." Alana smiles.

I will admit, it hurt knowing Alana chose someone else to be the maid of honor. But we also all agreed that it was better that she didn't pick one of us. We're all too close, and it's awkward to choose one friend over the other. Alana and Gemma were college roommates for years, so it made sense choosing her. She probably knew this version of Alana the best.

"Is Will bringing any single friends to the wedding?" I ask.

"I think all of his friends are already married." Alana frowns.

I nod. Sleeping with a man wasn't my favorite thing, but it had been so long since I'd slept with anyone. I've been wearing out my vibrator too many nights. At least I knew Wrenn couldn't hear that through the walls. And at least it was waterproof, because it was definitely getting fair use in the shower. Not like I have anyone specific to think about lately. I was usually so pent up by the time I was going to bed because of how Wrenn had been teasing me lately. It was bad enough she walked around half naked, but with the touching and the flirting, it made my body confused. Well, it confused my pussy. Maybe I just needed to sleep with someone and get her out of my head. But I couldn't even imagine bringing anyone else home.

"I'm teaching Kindergarten this year," Kim says, answering someone's question. I had zoned out of the conversation, but it doesn't seem like anyone noticed. I try to slip back in, undetected.

We split dessert; two orders of ice cream nachos split amongst us. By the time we're ready to go, I am stuffed. Heather decides to ride back with Norah, so I decide to take a drive by myself. I need to relax a bit before I go home. I don't know if Wrenn will be there and what she might be wearing. It seems like she gets closer and closer to walking around in the nude every day. Not that I'd mind.

But damn, that makes it that much harder to stay away from her. Wrenn is equally evil for teasing me as much as she was hot. I just want to take that mouth of hers and sit on her face. I can only imagine how good that would feel. Last year, we barely touched the surface hooking up. We went all the way, but it was a hazy memory. And I definitely didn't take control to sit on her face. All I remember was her surprising me by taking charge.

I drive toward town, without any destination in mind. Wrenn's tongue on me is the only thing I can think about right now. I clench my thighs together and groan. I wish she wasn't still so angry with me about last year. I wish I hadn't been such an idiot and ruined a good thing. I just didn't want it to get complicated and messy with us. But now here I am, horny as hell, avoiding going home just in case I might run into her.

The more she teases me, the more I tease back. We are always so close to the other breaking. Too many times now have I thought about saying fuck it and kissing her. But I don't want to make a move without knowing she is being serious about this. I can't risk my friendship with Alana again over a one-night stand with her sister.

TEN

Wrenn

I wake up in a sweat, turned on more than I care to admit. I had a sex dream about Ryleigh last night. The two of us hooking up in the pool. My pussy was soaked the second I woke up. Dragging my fingers down the front of my shorts, inside my panties, I feel how wet I am. Ugh. This isn't supposed to be happening. I'm supposed to be the one laughing, not over here, a sexually frustrated mess.

I grab my bullet vibe from the nightstand and click it on. Pressing it to my clit, I groan quietly. This time, I don't want Ryleigh hearing a sound from me. But I think about the other night, how good she looked as the sun was setting behind her. How fucking sexy she was when she took everything off. How freaking close I was to kissing her, just for a moment. She was temptation, and I was desperate for a taste.

Her naked body plays on repeat in my mind. Her fingers in my pussy, our bodies banging into each other as we kiss. The water splashing around us, only creating more sensations on our bodies. Ryleigh flicks her fingers over my clit, and in real life, I groan. I am so pent up that I am about to come any second. I steady my pace and let the orgasm take over. I'm seeing stars and biting down hard on my bottom lip. Finally, I relax and let go of the toy. I wipe it off on my T-shirt and toss it back in the drawer. Now I'm ready to start the day, which I usually start with a swim. But I'm not sure I should today.

No, I need my daily release. I always feel better when I swim and can clear my head before starting the day. So I grab one of my bathing suit bottoms and head for the pool. On the way out, I hear Ryleigh in the kitchen. She's cooking something with her back turned to me, so I manage to slip past her unnoticed.

I put my stuff on one of the chairs, then dive in the deep end. I close my eyes and swim back and forth from one end of the pool to the other. I need to get my laps in and relax a bit. I push everything from my mind while I swim. I don't need to think about Ryleigh or my sexy dream. No, right now all I needed was to *not* think. Eventually, I'm able to pull focus and just think about the water. Lap number thirty-seven. Lap number thirty-eight.

"Wrenn! I made lunch!" Ryleigh calls, snapping me out of my relaxing swim. I pause in the shallow end.

She's setting up some kind of food by the umbrella table. Rolling my eyes, I want to say no thanks. But my stomach is growling, and it does *look* good. I can always swim more later. Climbing out of the pool, I towel off just enough so I'm not dripping. Then I take a seat across from Ryleigh. I wait for her to blush when she realizes I'm topless. But she seems to be over that. Her eyes don't even linger below my collar bone. Huh. What's up with that?

"I made some pasta salad and sandwiches."

I look at the plate in front of me and peek at the ham and cheese sandwich next to the hearty helping of pasta salad.

"Looks good," I offer.

"I figured you might want something other than eggs and cereal." She smirks.

"Hey, I know how to make chicken Cesar wraps too."

"We really need to get you signed up for a cooking class."

"I don't know, I could get used to living with you if it means you'll cook for me, Princess." I wink, knowing that nickname seems to give her a reaction.

She clenches her jaw. "Why do you call me Princess?"

"Because I know it bothers you," I say with a shrug. I pick up a forkful of pasta and shove it in my mouth. Fuck, that is good.

"I'm hardly a Princess," she grumbles.

"Whatever you say…Princess." I smirk.

"Do you have work today?"

"Nope, it's my day off."

"Oh."

"Why? Tryna get rid of me?"

"No, I was going to paint out here today. But I don't want to be in the way."

"You're not in the way." I shrug.

"Oh okay."

"What are you painting?"

"I'm not sure yet. I have a few ideas, but I'll have to see what comes to me."

"Do you ever do portraits?" I ask.

"Sometimes, but it depends. I mainly like doing my own thing and selling it. It's less pressure and rules when I do it on my own," she explains.

"That makes sense." I nod.

"Are we actually having a conversation where you're not flirting with me?"

"I can't flirt and eat but give me five minutes and I'll turn it back on." I wink.

"There you are. I knew we couldn't get through a meal without that," she teases.

"Don't act like you don't love it."

Her silence only further proves my point.

"Don't you worry about being half naked all the time?"

"Why would I?" I frown, looking down.

"I don't know, what if you had a surprise guest?"

"Then they'd get an eyeful of my tits. And I doubt they'd ever surprise me again." I laugh.

"You're something else." She rolls her eyes as she finishes her lunch.

"Thank you. Feel free to paint out here. I'm going to tan until I can get back into the pool." I decide.

"Okay." She nods.

I help her bring the plates back in the house. Feeling her eyes on my ass while I walk puts a smirk on my face. I knew she couldn't help herself.

I slide on my sunglasses and grab a lounger by the pool. She couldn't see where I am looking but I am curious what she is painting today. Ryleigh takes her time taking the paints, her easel, and her supplies out of the room she usually paints in. She sets everything up meticulously before she takes a seat on her stool and stretches out her body. Raising her arms over her head, she cracks her knuckles and then looks at the empty canvas. I can't see what she's looking at, I'm not at the right angle for that.

So I flip onto my stomach to make sure my tan is even. There was nothing worse than an uneven tan. My eyes close and I let out a small yawn. With a full belly and the sun, I could fall asleep here. I listen to the quiet sounds the pool system makes, the splash of water each time Ryleigh cleans a brush, and the creaking of her stool as she rocks on it. After a while it feels relaxing, and I realize I can head back in the pool.

I start my laps, silence in my head as I swim the perimeter of the pool. Lap one. Lap two. My brain relaxes and I only stop once I hit fifty laps. I don't keep my abs by doing nothing. I work hard to get those babies and I want to keep them.

Ryleigh is still working when I get out of the pool. I walk over to her and stand behind her as she paints. She has the background of the painting almost done. It's the pool, the trees and the chairs in the backyard. I have to admit, she is incredibly talented. She manages to make it look almost lifelike on the canvas.

"Do you mind? You're dripping." Ryleigh shoots me a look, and I realize my hair is dripping pool water on her shoulder.

"Sorry, Princess." I wink and shake my head just a little bit more for her.

"Hey!" Ryleigh gets up, and I start running away.

I'm careful not to slip and fall. She chases me all the way toward the grassy area of the backyard. I laugh as she tries to get me. Eventually she catches up with me, and we both fall face forward into the grass in a fit of giggles. Her hands are all covered in blue paint, and I wrestle her hands to keep from getting on me. I'm holding her wrists away from my face while we roll around in the grass. I'm wet from the pool, so of course the grass is sticking to my body. Ryleigh's laughing until I end up straddling her, holding her wrists hostage over her head and my breasts close to her mouth.

"We should, um…" I let go of her hands and sit up a little straighter.

Except I'm on her lap, straddling her bare thighs. She brushes some of my hair out of my eyes, and I freeze. This feels more intimate than I anticipated. I can feel paint on my forehead now. Maybe that's all she was trying to do. But she's looking at my lips and fuck if I'm not tempted to lean in and let her kiss me.

"You should, uh, go rinse off, you're covered in grass," she says, clearing her throat.

"Oh, sure." I nod.

I slide off her lap and we both quietly walk back to the pool area. Ryleigh sits back down at the easel, and I head for the outdoor shower just to hose the dirt off me. I hate when grass and stuff gets into the pool. The water is freezing so I only stay under for a few minutes, enough to rinse off. Then I jump back in the pool. I can feel Ryleigh's eyes on me, but I don't give her the satisfaction of looking at her. I can't look at her right now. That was another close call. I'm supposed to be the one teasing her, but somehow she is getting more of a reaction out of me. Were my friends right? Do I have feelings for her? No, there's no way.

I watch Ryleigh paint after I feel her eyes fall off me. Her eyebrows are wrinkled together, her eyes determined to get this detail right. She paints purposefully. Each stroke is as important as the last. I can tell she's trying to get this part just right. I had no doubt it would come out amazing. I've seen her work over the years, and it is always incredible. When she's done, she puts the brush down, and I sneak over to see it again.

There in the middle of the pool painting is *me*. A topless, purple-haired woman with no face. But it is definitely me. Then an idea pops in my head. What if I had her paint me? She could have me pose and we could fool around in the paint after. Our hands and bodies a mess with the cool paint. Her handprints all over my body. I'd look like something off Pinterest.

"Paint me," I say aloud.

"What?" She faces me.

"You heard me. Paint me," I say, challenging her. It's a game of chicken and I'm determined to win.

"Why?"

"You probably need a muse of sorts, don't you? Let me be that."

"A muse is usually a love interest," she points out.

"So? Paint me anyway. Paint me on a canvas, paint my skin. Anything. I think it would be fun." I look her directly in the eyes so she can't look away from me. I can see the wheels turning in her creative mind as she considers it.

"I have always wanted to do a painting on someone's skin." She pauses.

"I have the best skin, smooth, tan. I'd be a great canvas." I smile. I do a little spin to show off my back, tossing my head over my shoulders to give her a look. I bat my eyelashes at her and smirk.

"Okay, I'll get skin safe paint." She heads inside, and I smile, knowing I have her right where I want her.

73

ELEVEN

Ryleigh

"I can paint anything?" I clarify as Wrenn lies down on the floor in the art room.

I suggested we come inside when I realized we might get paint everywhere. Now, with a painting cloth down on the hardwood floors, I feel more relaxed.

"Sure." She nods.

"Okay." I decide to start with a basic white layer for the background while I decide what I want to paint.

"Ooo, it's cold." She shudders as the paintbrush touches her bare skin.

"You can't move," I instruct.

She's quiet again as I paint the white rectangle on her back. I blow to dry it when I'm done. I notice the way she gets goosebumps on her skin. I wonder quietly if she is as horny as I am lately. But I push that thought from my mind. I decide to go with flowers. They are simple enough and easy to fix if I mess them up. Working on skin is different than paper and a canvas, so I'm not sure how this will go. I'm about to start when I realize the best place to get the best angle would be in between her thighs.

"Uh, I want to start, but the best angle is, well, between your legs."

"That's what she said." She laughs. "Go for it."

Wrenn spreads her thighs apart, and I suck in a breath. I'm careful not to lean on her ass as I start painting the outlines of the flowers. My thighs are touching hers as I sit on my knees to reach the top of her back. Squeezing them together, I pray she can't feel the heat radiating from them. I'm quiet as I try to focus on painting. I should have an Olympic medal for how well I'm focused on anything but her perky ass in my face.

"How's it going?" Wrenn asks.

"Great!" I chirp out in a squeakier tone than I expect. Great, now she'll know something is up.

"You okay? You seem a little tense."

"Nope, all good," I lie. My voice sounds steadier this time.

"That's too bad, I know the best thing for stress relief." I can feel her tempting me. My pussy drips into my panties and I stand up abruptly.

"I just need some water." I all but run to the kitchen, grab a fresh cup of water to drink and then splash some cool water on my cheeks. Fuck.

I return to Wrenn when I'm calmed down. But the moment I walk back in, I'm just as horny. Her body is perfect. The ass that doesn't quit, her long hair that I'm dying to wrap my hands in. Would one more night with her really be that bad?

"Ready?" She's laying on her side, tits exposed, and I know she's just doing that to tease me.

"Yup." I smile. Let's do this.

I get back into position between her thighs. But this time I do touch her ass. Just a light touch with the paintbrush, followed by a quick apology. She swallows hard and I continue painting her. I lean on the side where her hair is pushed to the side and blow just below her ear.

"Sorry, you had some fuzz," I lie.

"O-oh," she stutters. I've never been able to make her do that.

I know she is just as horny as me when she raises her ass to grind lightly into my pussy. I lean down in the paint, not caring that it's getting all over my clothes, and I pull her hair to the side. I grip it tightly, and Wrenn moans. She fucking *moans* as I pull it back and then let go.

"You okay?" I tease. I know she has to be as wet as I am. But I'm not giving in first.

"Yup. Never better." But she clenches her thighs under me, so I brush the side of her hips.

I can feel her struggling to fight this. I am seconds away from flipping her over and eating her out right now. But at the last second, she flips over and grabs me by the throat.

"Two can play at this, Princess." She smirks.

I don't care anymore. Her breasts are perky, her pink nipples standing at attention with the metal bars begging to be played with. I needed to fuck her, and I needed to fuck her now.

"Truce," I say quietly.

"Truce." She nods.

Then our lips touch. I couldn't tell you who makes the first move because we're all hands and tongues. Her nipples are under my painted thumbs while her tongue is in my mouth. She tastes like cherries. Wrenn's hands are on my ass, and I swear we've been wasting time not doing this. She flips me with her legs so she can be on top. The paints I had on the side spill all over us but neither of us care to stop. The cool paint covers my T-shirt which prompts Wrenn to take it off me.

"Fuck, I've been dying to see those tits." She moans as she raises the T-shirt over my head.

I'm not wearing a bra, so she dips her head down to my breast and takes my nipple in her mouth. She scrapes her teeth over my nipple. It should hurt, but I only cry out in pleasure. My skin feels electric with each touch. I'm like a firework ready to be set off.

"Just fuck me already." I moan. I don't have patience for foreplay. I want to be *fucked*.

"In due time, Princess." She smirks.

Wrenn runs a hand under my shorts and stops over the wet

spot on my panties. I suck in a breath as she slowly trails her fingers over the spot. When she presses down with two fingers, I gasp as she touches my clit.

"Such a needy girl." She's having too much fun with this.

"I bet you're just as wet," I challenge. My hand goes for her bottoms, but she stops me.

"I'm in charge."

She slides off my shorts and panties in one swoop. Then she pins my wrists to the ground and shimmies her body down until her face is at my pussy. Finally, I'm going to get some action. I feel like a teenage boy on the verge of exploding. Wrenn blows softly on my pussy, causing me to shiver in anticipation. She slides her hand up my slit and dances her fingers around my clit.

"Oh." My hips buck against her touch, but she pushes them back down.

Taking her fingers off me, she puts them to her lips and sucks on them. God, why was that so fucking hot? I wanted her to taste me.

"Sweet," she murmurs.

I'm about to protest when she presses her face to my pussy. Her tongue connects with my clit, and I moan her name. Oh my gosh. It's even better than I remembered it to be. Wrenn flattens her tongue and slides it down my slit, gathering all the wetness on her tongue before circling back to the clit. My hands grab her dark hair, holding her head steady. I tangle my fingertips in her wet locks.

"Mmm," she hums against me.

I need her to keep going, to finish me off. Her hand reaches for my breast, taking my nipple between her fingers. She plays with it roughly, and I gasp. Her wet hair drips on my thighs as her tongue circles my clit again. She uses her free hand to slide a finger inside me. Her tongue on my sensitive bud makes me cry out. I can feel the orgasm building, and I'm seconds away from begging for it. Fuck, we called a truce. I have nothing to lose.

"God! Right there!" I call out. I don't want her to stop.

Wrenn keeps going, and I feel my legs shake as my vision goes black. I explode for her, my pussy squirting all over her fingers and face. I don't care, I'm letting everything go. She doesn't stop until I push her face away. I'm gasping for air when she stands and grabs my cup of water.

"Here, drink." She sits down, holding my cup to my lips, and I take it from her. The water quenches my thirst and gives me a second to breathe normally again.

"I didn't peg you for a squirter, Princess." She smirks as she looks me over. I feel like I'm on display as she lets her gaze drop all over my body. But I don't feel self-conscious, I know what I have to offer is good.

"It doesn't always happen." I shrug.

"I must be special then," she says smugly. I have a feeling she isn't going to let this go.

"Or I was just horny."

"Either way, it's because of me."

I can't even argue with her. She is right.

I put the cup of water down and pull her in for a kiss. I need to taste her again. But her lips taste mostly of me, and I blush. Why does that turn me on even more? I grab her breasts, playing with her piercings, and she moans in my mouth.

"I want to taste you," I mutter against her lips.

"Only if I can have another taste."

She slides off the bathing suit bottoms, tossing them to the side, and slides her body toward me. I position myself under her between her legs as she lowers her pussy on my face. She tastes even better than I remember. Sweet and delicious. I run my tongue through her folds and hum lightly.

Wrenn bends forward, grabs my ass, and pushes her tongue into my pussy. My body is still sensitive as hell, but Wrenn doesn't care. Her tongue is working its magic to make me come, and I have to remind myself to focus on her. I want to make her come just as hard. Everything seems to be a competition with her. So while I swirled my tongue over her clit, she darts hers inside me, and I moan against her. I hold her hips steady, then smack her ass *hard*.

"Oh, Princess." Wrenn gasps.

I hit her ass again, this time harder. She moans again and I know with how wet she is, it's only spurring her on. I dig my nails in her ass cheeks and let my tongue run over her core.

"Fuck," I mutter as she slides two fingers inside me.

She is not going to make me come for a second time without me making her come at least once. Her heavy breathing against my pussy only spurs me on as I slide my tongue over her clit. I suck hard on it, and she shoots to sitting up. She stops eating me out to start riding my face. She is chasing a quick release, and I'm going to get her there.

"Fuck! Yes! Don't stop!" she screams out. I suck on her clit as her pussy moves quickly over my lips. She's close, I can tell by the way she's tensing up. So I slap her ass one last time.

"Yesssss!" Wrenn squeals, and I don't stop. She rides her hips over my face until her legs give out and she falls next to me.

"Holy fuck," she mutters quietly.

I smile proudly. I knew I could, but it still feels good when you get someone off that well. Wrenn lays next to me, catching her breath. She's never looked hotter. Her purple curls sprawled around her, her body covered in red and white paint. She looks like she went swimming in my art supplies. I imagine if someone found us like this. I'm sure they'd be too stunned to speak. Wrenn is quiet, like both of us are afraid to speak. Was the truce over? Was this a one-time thing? I had way too many questions spiraling around in my head.

TWELVE

Wrenn
______

"I'm all sticky." I groan, looking at the paint all over me.

"I am too." Ryleigh blushes. The red dancing across her cheeks makes me smile.

"Come shower with me," I decide.

Standing up, I grab her hand and lead her to my bedroom. Cheeto isn't around so I turn on the water and shut the door behind us. I don't want Cheeto trying to join us or something.

"Come on." I hold open the curtain for her and Ryleigh steps inside under the water.

I climb in behind her and try to get under the warm water. The shower head is strong but it wasn't very big, so we had to stand chest to chest to both get water from it. But her nipples brush against mine and my piercings, so I let out a moan. Ryleigh's eyes flicker to mine, and then her lips are on mine, soft and sweet. I slip my tongue inside to play with hers. Ryleigh's hands are on my hips, and I wrap my arms around her neck.

"I need you again," she admits.

"Tell me what you want, Princess." I smirk. I love hearing her ask for it.

"I want you to finger me. Make me come again," Ryleigh says.

"Again? Your pretty little pussy hasn't had enough yet?" I trail my hand down to her pussy and brush lightly on her lips.

"Y-yess." She bucks under my touch. God, she is so fucking sensitive.

"I want to hear you say my name when you come. Okay?" I touch her clit and she curses.

"Okay." She nods furiously. "Just quit teasing."

"Teasing is the best part, Princess." I wink before sliding a finger inside her warm center.

Ryleigh loses her balance, leaning against me for support. I lean forward and start kissing her ear. I nibble on her earlobe as I pump my finger in and out of her dripping wet pussy. She's panting hard in my ear, and I know I could do whatever I wanted with her right now. There was a certain power in being the one in charge of someone else's orgasm that I *loved*. I relished in being in charge of Ryleigh.

Leaning forward, I bite gently on her neck, and she gasps. I slide a second finger inside her and pump harder. She's tight, swallowing my fingers as I curl them to hit her G-spot.

"Wrenn!" She moans.

"Keep going, Princess." I coach her.

I kiss her neck, placing soft kisses. Then I suck on the nape of her neck, and she leans into me. Her moans get louder as I suck harder. I want to leave my mark on her. I pump my fingers in and out of her pussy, and I can feel her getting closer.

"Right there!" she calls out, and I flick my thumb over her clit to send her over the edge.

I move to another spot on her neck, then suck again as she comes all over my hand.

"Wrenn! Oh fuck! Wrenn!" Ryleigh screams, and it's like music to my ears. It is nice knowing you had your enemy right where you want her.

Sure, the plan wasn't to sleep with her. But I was horny and she was offering, it wasn't like I gave in first. Now all I need to do was ghost her the way she ghosted me. Sure, it might be harder living under the same roof. But it could be done. It had to be.

"Fuck, that was so good." Ryleigh stands up straighter.

I raise the temperature of the water and pick up my loofah. I pour a hearty amount of soap on it and start scrubbing my body. I need to get all this paint off me before we go to bed. Ryleigh takes the washcloth on the hook and starts doing the same. We take turns rinsing off before we start on our hair. At least we manage to keep the paint out of our hair or that would've been a nightmare. I use my color-safe shampoo and offer Ryleigh some of my normal one.

"Shit, I don't have a towel," Ryleigh realizes as we're about to get out.

"I'll dry off and go grab yours."

"Thanks." She smiles.

I take my towel off the hook, grab my robe, and head to her room after drying off. Ryleigh's towel is hanging on the back of her bathroom. When I return, Ryleigh is still in the shower rinsing off. I shut off the water, hand her the towel, and then walk into my room.

What the hell is going to happen now? Is she going to sleep in here? Is she going to put on clothes and go to bed? Will we talk about it? I really hope we won't, but I have a feeling she might try to. I probably should've thought about this before I offered her to shower with me. But I was dirty, and I wasn't ready for our night to be done.

"I'm gonna go grab some clothes," Ryleigh says, wrapped in her towel. I nod, and she disappears out the door.

Now what? Is she coming back? Should I get dressed? I decide to put on my sexiest pajamas. A pair of silk shorts and a silky tank top. It is comfortable and I know it shows off all my assets. I decide to put the TV on in case she comes back. Then maybe she won't try to talk about what happened, and if she wants to, she could join in.

Ryleigh appears in the doorway a few minutes later in an

oversized T-shirt and fuzzy socks. She'd look cozy if it weren't for the red lacy panties sticking out from under the shirt. Maybe tonight isn't over.

"Wrenn Thomas! Do you know what you did to my *neck*!?" Ryleigh squeals pushing her hair out of the way. Sure enough, there are two bright purple bruises forming on the side of her neck.

"I like to brand what's mine." I shrug.

"Yours?" She growls.

"Come watch a movie." I change the subject.

"Movie?" she asks, looking at the TV.

"Thought I'd start one, you can join." I pat the bed next to me, and she smiles.

This is perfect. She can spend the night in my bed, and in the morning I'll sneak out before she wakes up. Then I can avoid her for the rest of time, and she'll know exactly how it feels.

"What are we watching?" Ryleigh lays down on my pillow, and I smell my shampoo on her. Her warm scent is mixed with the guava shampoo.

"Twilight."

"Oh god." Ryleigh groans.

"It's my comfort movie." If ever a time I needed it, it was now.

"Fine."

I lie down on the pillows and Ryleigh shifts next to me. We aren't cuddling, but if either of us moved a centimeter, we'd be touching. I'm not used to having people stay the night. Especially someone like Ryleigh. I move my hand to grab the remote and it falls between the headboard and the bed behind me. It happens a lot because of the gap there, so I bend on my knees to reach down and grab it. I'm picking it up when I feel a hand on my ass.

"Excuse me?" I smirk, turning around.

"Well, if you're gonna show it off." She smiles.

I toss the remote on my nightstand and then look back at

Ryleigh. She's smiling, but her cheeks are a bright red, giving away exactly what she wants right now.

"You can't get enough of me, can you Princess?" I say smugly.

"Oh whatever." She rolls her eyes and playfully touches my shoulder.

I lean in and press my lips softly to hers. But as soon as I do, I get a hunger for more. She kisses me fiercely, her tongue swiping over my bottom lip. We fight for control but ultimately, she gives in, and I climb on her lap. When I'm straddling her waist, she grabs my ass and squeezes. Her lips melt into mine, my hands roam under her T-shirt to find her breasts. God, the way they fit perfectly in my hands. I flick her nipple and tug on her bottom lip with my teeth.

"Ohh." She moans into my mouth. She likes it when I'm rough with her.

I grind my hips against hers and play with her tits. Ryleigh is in my bed, and I can't pretend like this isn't a dream. A dream I've been having a lot lately. I start kissing her neck again when she pulls back.

"Be careful with the markings," she warns.

"I seem to recall you like the way they felt when I was leaving them." I smirk.

Before she can respond, I bite on her neck. It's a soft bite, but then I suck and she moans for me. There's definitely going to be a new mark but I don't see her stopping me. If anything, she's only encouraging me with her moans and whimpers.

"You look so sexy when I brand you." I smirk.

Ryleigh groans but holds back a smile. She kisses me harder, grabbing my waist and pulling me into her. Like she suddenly can't get enough of me. She spreads her legs, and my thigh falls between hers. Instantly, she pushes her pussy against it and starts grinding. She's humping my fucking leg, trying to get herself off again.

"Does Princess want to come again?" I tease.

"God, yes." She groans.

"Why don't you ask nicely then?"

"Please can you make me come?" She rolls her eyes.

"Try again." I cup my hand on her pussy. "This time, I want you to beg."

"Oh, fuck. Please fuck me, Wrenn. Please. I'm so fucking horny." She whimpers.

I smile. Sliding her panties to the side, I flick my thumb across her clit, and she gasps. So sensitive, so sweet. I put my two fingers near her mouth.

"Open and suck," I tell her. She sucks on my fingers, wetting them with her spit. Then I slide them inside her pussy.

"Yes!" She gasps.

Ryleigh rides my hand, her body tightening around my fingers. She's so wet my fingers almost fall out a few times. But I persist. I'm determined to make her come so hard she'll fall asleep. I kiss her neck, careful of the new bruises. Biting on her bottom lip, I look into her eyes as I let it go. She leans in to kiss me, but I tease her. Soft and slow kisses, the opposite of what she wants. I edge her, making her wait for what she really wants.

"Please," she cries out.

I push my fingers in harder and look at her.

"Play with your clit," I command. Her hand instantly drops to her pussy. She's rubbing quick circles over her clit.

Ryleigh moans, and her pussy clenches around my fingers. I can feel her orgasm coming, so I kiss her hard. My mouth takes control, sucking gently on her tongue. I pull away as she calls out my name. God, who knew it could sound so good coming off her tongue?

Ryleigh falls back into the bed, wet hair everywhere, a slumped mess. Her eyes flutter closed, and she lets out a small yawn. I smile, knowing my work here is done. I grab a tissue for my fingers and try to lay down when Ryleigh pulls me toward her. I think she's going to kiss me until she wraps her arms around me, and I rest my head on her chest.

I didn't expect to cuddle with her. But I guess I have to make this believable. Besides, her boobs do make a nice pillow. I suppose one night can't hurt. I'll just make sure to get out of bed before her. It won't be that hard. I'm usually up before her most mornings anyway. I'll slip out and this will all be my sweet revenge. Closing my eyes, I yawn and try not to get too comfortable.

THIRTEEN

Ryleigh

"**W**RENN! RYLEIGH! I NEED YOU!" Alana's voice carries throughout the house. I peek open one eye, expecting to see my nightstand. But instead, I see purple hair and a tan face sleeping next to me.

Am I still in Wrenn's room? I sit up with a start. Oh fuck, I fell asleep here last night. One too many orgasms, and I was out like a light. Wrenn is sleeping peacefully when I hear Alana's voice again. So I wasn't dreaming that. FUCK. She's about to find me in her little sister's bed.

"WRENN! RYLEIGH! WHERE ARE YOU?" Alana's voice gets louder, which can only mean she's getting closer.

"Wrenn! Wake up! Alana's here," I whisper-yell. She doesn't move, so I push her shoulder a few times until she groans.

"Alana's here. GET UP." I jump out of bed, but it's no use. I'm in pajamas, there's no lying about what I'm doing in here.

"Fuck," Wrenn mutters as she gets up.

"Wrenn, I don't care if you're sleeping or you're naked, I'm coming in!" Alana shouts. "There you are! What are you both doing in here…" She looks confused between us but then waves us off. "Never mind, we have bigger issues."

"What happened?" I sit on the edge of the bed, trying to hide the fact that I'm not wearing any shorts.

"I thought I could do this alone. I had everything all planned out but now it's all ruined and it's too late to hire a wedding planner. What am I going to do?" Alana starts crying. Which, if you know Alana, it's incredibly unlike her. I think I've only seen her cry one other time, at her grandmother's funeral.

"What's ruined?" Wrenn rubs her eyes.

"The centerpieces came but they aren't put together like they should've been. The name cards aren't complete, and the invitations aren't sent. It was supposed to be done already, but I entrusted Will to do the invites and he *forgot*."

"He forgot?" I gasp.

"I give the man one job and he forgets," Alana grumbles. She wipes the tears from her eyes and sighs. "Anyway, it's all a mess, and I really need your help. Everyone else is busy today, I called on the way over. I actually called you guys too, but no one answered."

"My phone is dead," I lie. I think it's still somewhere in the art room.

Oh fuck. The art room looks like a mess. Wrenn and I had left it a mess when we went to shower. I thought I'd clean it up today but there's no way I can with Alana here. But she also can't see it. I'm pretty sure there are a few ass and breast prints in the paint that I can't explain.

"I have stuff in my car."

"Why don't you go get it and I'll make coffee, and then we can help in any way we can," I suggest.

"Okay." Alana looks a little bit relieved.

The second she leaves the room, I look at Wrenn. We need to talk about what happened last night but now is *not* the time. We can't have a real conversation until we're alone again. So for now, I need to pretend like I didn't just sleep with my best friends little sister. Which is easier said than done.

I run to my room, put on a fresh pair of clothes, and then

head to the kitchen. Alana is bringing in the last of her stuff when I flip the coffee machine on. It's only nine a.m., but it feels like three a.m. with how little sleep I got last night.

"Can I have an extra shot of expresso in mine?" Alana asks.

"Coming right up."

"I'll help, but I'm having breakfast first," Wrenn says as she walks into the kitchen.

"Fine." Alana nods.

I hand Alana a cup of coffee and her eyes pop open. "Is that a hickey?!"

"Uh, yeah." My hand goes to cover my neck, but I know it's useless.

"Details, please? I thought you weren't seeing anyone."

"Uh, I'm not. It just sort of happened," I say.

"Who is she? Or he?" Alana asks as she sips the coffee.

"Just someone. No one you know," I lie.

"Interesting. Well, let me know if they're coming to the wedding."

"Will do." I nod. I can't explain they already have an invite to the wedding. In the corner of the kitchen, Wrenn smirks smugly into her cereal.

"So, I need you to write out the place cards because you're an artist with the neatest handwriting." Alana hands me a stack of white cards and a calligraphy pen. "And you have to help me with the center pieces," she says, turning to Wrenn.

"Gross, okay," Wrenn grumbles.

"Happy to help." I smile.

I take a seat next to Alana and look at the cards she's already done. Only some of them have names, like the person making them got tired halfway through. She hands me the list of names and I decide to practice on the back. It's been a while since I've done any calligraphy. It is one of my many talents, but sometimes it takes me a minute to remember it perfectly. I write the alphabet on the back, have Alana check it over, and then start.

"You guys are so quiet it's making me anxious. What's going on?" Alana asks suddenly.

"I just don't wanna mess this up," I lie.

"I'm still half asleep." Wrenn shrugs.

"Did you work last night?"

"Yeah," Wrenn lies.

"Have you seen Shelly again?" Alana asks ,and my hand runs off the card, leaving a black line in the middle of Heather's name.

"I'm so sorry."

"It's okay, there should be a few extra," Alana reassures me and then turns back to Wrenn.

"Uh no." Wrenn looks at her awkwardly.

"Who's Shelly?" I ask, trying not to sound like a jealous girlfriend.

"You know Shelly. She and Wrenn were attached at the hip for years! Her ex-girlfriend," Alana explains.

"Oh right. I didn't know you guys were seeing each other again." I was definitely failing at acting cool right now.

"We're not. My sister thinks we are." Wrenn rolls her eyes.

"Because they hooked up," Alana sings.

I grip the pen tightly, taking it off the paper this time. *Shelly* was her loud *friend*?

"It was nothing." Wrenn avoids eye contact with me.

Whatever. It's not like Wrenn and I are something. She can fuck whoever she wants. But why does that make me want to claw that girl's eyes out? It isn't her fault. The sounds of her moans fill my ears as I think about that night. Knowing who it was just makes it a million times worse.

"I still think you should bring her to the wedding, you never know what could happen." Alana smiles. Of course she has no idea she's causing me physical pain.

"Please just drop it." Wrenn glances at me for just a second. But I look away, I'm sure my face is giving away everything.

"Alright, well I have to get the rest of the phone numbers for the florists. I'll be right back." Alana hops off the chair and heads outside.

"So, Shelly huh?" I can't help myself.

"It's really nothing," Wrenn says.

"Is she your loud *friend*?"

"Yes." Wrenn grimaces.

I don't know what to say. Wrenn and I hooked up once a year ago and once last night. It's not like I have some kind of a claim on her. We are both single and can do whatever or whomever we want. I just hate the idea of Wrenn being with someone else. It feels like a punch to my throat. We both stay quiet until Alana comes back in, letting her guide the conversation for the rest of the afternoon.

"So, the girls and I are going to stuff the wedding invites tomorrow. Do you think we can do that here?" Alana asks, looking between Wrenn and I.

"Sure. No problem." I smile.

"Whatever, as long as there's booze." Wrenn shrugs.

"We're having *brunch*. But yes, mimosas will be served." Alana nods.

"Is mom coming?"

"No, she and Dad went away for the weekend."

"What? No one told me. Where did they go?" Wrenn frowns.

"They went to Cape Cod for the weekend. I think it was pretty spur of the moment," Alana says.

Wrenn grumbles, and I quietly write names on the cards. If you knew Alana's parents, you'd know they didn't do anything spontaneously. They planned everything down to the minute of the day. We were allowed to have sleepovers on the third Saturday of the month but not any others. We hung out at Alana's house on Wednesday nights because that was her parents date night. But not on anniversaries unless you wanted to catch them having sex. Which Alana apparently did, more than once. As someone who's caught their parents doing it, it's worth years in therapy.

Alana's phone starts ringing, and she excuses herself to the dining room to take it. She returns less than three minutes later looking more frazzled than before.

"What's wrong?" I ask.

"Will's mother just told me I can't have a DJ play at the reception because she already booked some jazz band she and his dad like," Alana grumbles.

"What the fuck? It's not their wedding," Wrenn speaks up.

"I know, but they're paying for it. So Will thinks we should just go for it." Alana sighs.

"If he doesn't stick up for you now, will he ever stand up to his mother? I swear he's more of a mama's boy than anyone we know," Wrenn teases.

"He's not that bad," Alana argues.

"If he could still breastfeed from her, he totally would," Wrenn says.

"Shut up!" Alana tosses a plastic flower at Wrenn's head.

"I'm just saying, Will should be standing up to his mom. Not delivering bad news on the phone."

"You're right. I just don't want to fight; it seems like lately there's so much fighting going on." Alana sighs.

"With you and Will?"

"Yeah. We're both overworked and stressed about the wedding. We have so much family coming in and stuff going on. I think it'll calm down once the stress of the day is over," Alana says unconvincingly.

I'm not sure what to say. I've only met Will a handful of times and honestly, he seems okay. Like there's nothing wrong with him, but it also surprises me this is the kind of guy Alana ended up with. Not that he isn't her type, he just seems so plain. Before him, she dated all kinds of guys. A book cover model, a tattoo artist, even a corrections officer. But Will is just a banker who went to business school and followed in the family business. Alana is exciting and fun where Will is just boring. But Alana seems happy, so that's what matters. Maybe it's one of those situations where opposites attract or something. Lately, it just seems like something more was going on. She didn't say exactly what it was, but I could read between the lines.

I've never been married, and the only one of our group who actually has been married is Norah. But she never acted like this with her late husband, Finn. You couldn't separate those two with a crow bar. They were inseparable from the day they met. I truly believe he was her soul mate. I know everyone is different, but it just seems like there's something off with Will and Alana.

But I stay silent, not wanting to rock the boat. Especially this close to the wedding. Alana has enough stress to deal with. I don't want her to think I don't like her fiancé or something. I just hope it will work itself out for the better. My best friend deserves the wedding of her dreams with a happy ending.

FOURTEEN

Wrenn

I pour myself another mimosa as I try to block out the nagging voice telling me I don't belong. I'm a grown up, and I'm still carrying around the insecurities from my youth. My sister invited her friends over and I was instantly back to being the odd one out. I'm sure they didn't mean it now. It wasn't like when we were younger, and I was purposely kept out. It was just hard knowing I didn't understand their jokes and will never fully fit in with them.

Maybe if I wasn't avoiding Ryleigh, I'd have a better chance at fitting in. But from the moment I woke up this morning to just minutes before the party started, all Ryleigh wanted to do was talk. That awkward, "what are we" conversation you have after a one-night stand. She was determined to have it with me, while I was determined to avoid it for as long as possible.

Since I didn't wake up early enough to ghost her yesterday, plus my sister kept us in the same room for majority of the day until I had work, I never got the chance to sneak out on her like she did to me so now it was even more awkward. Would we be doing it again? Were we friends? What would my sister think? I knew all the things she wanted to talk to me about. Which is why I'm on my third mimosa and planned to be drunk by the time this thing is over.

"Wrenn! Come help with the invites," Alana tells me.

I walk into the dining room with my drink in hand. The girls are all stuffing, labeling, and sealing the wedding invitations like an assembly line. But of course, there's only one seat left next to Ryleigh.

"Come sit next to Ryleigh, she doesn't bite," Heather says with a smile.

Ryleigh blushes a deep red that only I notice. At least today, she's covered up the proof of our hookup on her neck with some concealer. The last thing we need is her friends bugging her about who marked up her neck. I didn't have confidence that she'd be able to keep it a secret.

I take a seat next to Ryleigh and Alana hands me a roll of stamps and the stack of wedding invites. I guess my job was simple enough. I could stick some stamps on some envelopes and call it a day.

"When you're done with those, there's more." Alana smiles.

"How many people are you inviting?" I raise an eyebrow at her.

"Uh, five hundred was the last count. But I'm not sure. Mom and Dad and Will's parents keep giving us new people to invite." She frowns.

"Shit." Ryleigh mumbles next to me.

"Wasn't Will supposed to be helping out?" I ask.

"Yeah. But he had work so…" Her voice trails and I sigh. The more I learn about my future brother-in-law, the less I like. He just made my sister so passive aggressive. It was like this was his wedding, not *theirs*.

"Don't give her a hard time," Ryleigh whispers to me when Alana disappears to the kitchen.

"I'm not."

Ryleigh shoots me a look, but I stick my tongue out at her. It's immature, but I'm a little tipsy, and I can't say anything else right now. She shakes her head, and the girls start a conversation about something else. I don't know what they're talking about, so I focus on placing the stamps. Alana wants everything to be perfect, so I make sure each one is on straight in the corner.

"Any plans on the bachelorette party?" Heather asks quietly.

"Gemma and Ry are planning it last I heard," Norah says.

"I need her number actually; we haven't finalized anything," Ryleigh adds.

"Here, I'll send it to you." Norah smiles.

"Are you guys getting her a stripper?" I ask. Kim and Norah choke on their drinks and Heather smiles at me.

"We are, but don't tell her," Ryleigh says quietly.

"I can't wait to see that." I laugh. My sister with a *stripper*? She's going to have a freaking heart attack.

"She's going to freak out," Kim mumbles. She's a teacher and from what I know about her, she's almost as modest as Alana.

"It's not like she's never seen a dick," I add. All their eyes are on me like I've cursed in church.

"Maybe you've had enough," Ryleigh says quietly, eyeing my mimosa. But I'm not even drunk yet.

I ignore her, grabbing my glass and chugging the rest of it.

"Don't you have work later?" Ryleigh asks.

Fuck. I forgot I have work today. I don't want to give Ryleigh the satisfaction of being right.

"Why is everyone quiet?" Alana asks walking back in.

"Your friends are prudes." I smirk.

"Are you drunk?" Alana frowns.

"I'm tipsy. I could probably still do a handstand." I shrug.

"She has work today," Ryleigh adds, and I glare at her. Hasn't she done enough?

"Shit. I can't drive her in." Alana looks at her phone and starts typing away.

All of her friends came in the car with her so it wasn't like one of them could drive me. Alana must have the same thought process. Everyone else goes back to small talk and envelope stuffing, but I can feel Ryleigh's eyes on me.

"Can you go to work tipsy?" Ryleigh asks quietly.

"It's more fun that way." I giggle.

"She can, it's not like she's doing brain surgery. She works at a bar," Alana adds.

"Maybe you should have some bread, I think there's a croissant left," Heather says with a smile.

"Ooo." I stand up and honestly, I might be drunk. Because I'm definitely light on my feet and all the alcohol in my system goes to my brain as I stand up.

I find the croissant on a plate in the kitchen. I'm taking the last bite when Alana comes in.

"Go get dressed for work, Ryleigh said she'll take you."

"What?"

"Get dressed. Ryleigh is taking you to work."

"Why can't you do it?" I groan.

"Because I have a million things to do today. Ryleigh doesn't mind."

"I just. I'll just call out."

"No, you let a little loose. You'll be sober within the hour, and you'll be fine."

"Ugh, fine." I groan.

Turning the corner I almost run into Ryleigh. Fuck. She probably heard me complaining to Alana. I don't mind it, but I don't want to be alone with her right now. I'm not sober enough for this conversation. But who knew when we'd be alone again. Last night Alana ended up spending the night on the couch. Of course, she went home to change and put herself together. Sometimes I hated how much of a show my sister put on lately.

I dash to my room and look for something to wear to work. I toss my dress aside and slide on jeans and a crop top. I slip my phone in my back pocket. I'm on the hunt for my sneakers, which I find by the door and Ryleigh.

"Ready?" She smiles.

"Yup." I nod. I slide on my sunglasses; it was bound to be way too bright out here.

"Do you need a ride home too?" Ryleigh asks as she turns on the AC in her car.

"Nah, I'll have one of my friends come get me." I need to avoid Ryleigh starting after work.

"Are you sure? I don't mind."

"Yeah, it's cool," I insist.

Part of me feels bad. Ryleigh is so nice. But why hadn't she been last time? Why had she fucked me and didn't even give me the courtesy of a text back? I didn't think just because we hooked up once that we were going to fall in love. But Ryleigh and I had been somewhat of friends before that. So to lose the start of something hurt worse. She didn't even give me a chance.

Ryleigh's quiet, and I'm grateful it's a quick drive to the bar. My leg is shaking. I couldn't help it, I felt anxious as hell and wanted to get out of here. I didn't want to say something stupid and regret it because she brings up something big like that.

"I'll keep my phone on in case you change your mind," Ryleigh says as we pull up.

"What?" I look at her quizzically.

"In case you need a ride home?"

"Right, okay. Thanks." I slip out of the car, closing the door behind and head into the bar.

I say my hello's and start brewing a cup of coffee. I'm going to need it if I have to get sober at work. I should've snuck some alcohol of my own in. Not that I can't help myself to what was here. But I don't know how it would be if my boss came in. Or if they checked the cameras that I wasn't sure they had installed. I tie on my apron on my waist and then turn to the bar.

The familiar brown hair at the end of the bar catches my eye. I make my way to the end and look at Ryleigh. "Can I help you?"

"Yeah, can I have a cup of coffee?"

"What? Why?" I frown. She wants a cup of coffee? I was

about to drink the dirt they call coffee because I had to. Why would she choose a cup from *here*?

"I'll be here a bit. Until you sober up."

"You can't be serious." I scoff. "I don't need a babysitter. In case you've forgotten, I'm a consenting adult now."

"I didn't forget. I just thought you could use some company while you sober up." Ryleigh blushes hard.

"I'm fine."

"I know. And I know you can handle yourself. But it doesn't hurt to let someone be here." Ryleigh sighs. I roll my eyes. How could I argue with that.

"Fine. But I can't talk much, this is my job," I insist.

"Understandable." She nods.

"Also, the coffee is trash here. Do you want milkshake instead? I'm good at those."

"Okay." Ryleigh smiles.

I grab the empty glasses off the bar, check on the other patrons, and chug two cups of the coffee. I take shots of milk as a chaser. I grab the chocolate ice cream, rainbow sprinkles, and whipped cream from the bank. I start mixing enough for two shakes. If she's having one ,so am I. Making it fancy with the whipped cream and sprinkles, I use almost the rest of the can.

"Shit, this does look good," Ryleigh praises as I hand her the milkshake.

I pick up the whipped cream can and hold it to my mouth. I let the rest of the whipped cream fall on my tongue. Ryleigh clenches her jaw and I lick my lips clean.

"Be careful, you're going to lose some of that milkshake," I tease, pointing to her lip.

"You're going to give that guy an orgasm," Ryleigh whispers back.

I turn to the man who does look like he's going to burst. His eyes are almost as big as his head. I blow him a kiss and wave before turning back to Ryleigh.

"God, you're such a flirt." She rolls her eyes.

"I thought that's what you liked about me, Princess." I wink.

Ryleigh stares at me like she wants to protest but isn't sure what to say. I love how much my nickname gets her hot and bothered. Mostly bothered, but I'm pretty sure if I called her that in bed she'd ask to sit on my face. Not that I'd be complaining. Fuck, I thought all my sexual thoughts about her would be gone once I hooked up with her again. But the more I think about her, the more I want another taste.

FIFTEEN

Ryleigh

Wrenn flirts with me, even when the alcohol she had is out of her system. If I didn't know any better, I'd think she was trying to get back in my pants. And I hate even more to admit that it might be working. She's just so fucking charming when she wants to be. She'd chugged a few cups of coffee and downed the milkshake quicker than I had. Then she brought over a plate of French fries when it was getting late. I know she gets out of work late, and I'm thankful she let me stay.

"I just need to lock up, can I meet you at the car?" she asks, wiping down the bar.

"Sure." I nod.

It's dark, but the lights in the parking lot make it feel less creepy. I walk over to the car and get in the driver's seat. Two minutes later, Wrenn is climbing inside too.

"Is my sister still at home?" she asks.

"I don't know. She wasn't thrilled when I told her I was staying to make sure you were okay at work."

"You didn't have to stay."

"I know." I sigh. I hate that I had *wanted* to.

I'm not usually the gushy type when it came to hookups. I'm

the hit it and quit it type. If last year with Wrenn was any indication, I rarely did relationships. But this time with Wrenn feels different somehow. It's like suddenly I don't mind being around her. It's annoying as fuck. Which is why I want to talk to Wrenn about what happened so we can both move on. I can't ghost her this time while living in the same house and with the wedding coming up. But I can't go on with this inkling of a crush either.

Wrenn and I walk into the house, and she calls out Alana's name. There's no answer, and she disappears into the dining room where everyone was earlier.

"They seem to be gone. They even cleaned up when they left," Wrenn says, impressed.

"That's good." I kick off my sneakers and I'm about to head to bed when Wrenn stops me.

"Are you going to bed?"

"I was thinking about it."

"I might have a better offer." She smirks.

"What did you have in mind?"

"Maybe a repeat of the other night?"

"Who says I want that?" I counter. Wrenn's face drops, just for a second but enough for me to catch it.

"I'm pretty sure you do, Princess."

"Sure enough to play me for it?"

"Play you how?" She looks confused.

"Strip poker. If I win, you have to stop calling me Princess."

"And if I win?" She raises a brow.

"If you win you can do whatever you want to me."

"Whatever?"

"*Whatever.*"

I walk into the kitchen feeling more confident than I have all day. If she wants me, she has to win me. I dig in the junk drawer to grab the playing cards I know I saw. Wrenn's waiting on the couch in the living room.

"Do you know how to play poker?" I ask, taking a seat across from her.

"Yes." She rolls her eyes.

"I'll deal then." I proudly shuffle the cards up and hand them out.

Wrenn looks serious and focused as we play. She barely looks at me, like she's afraid of giving something away. I'm sure my face gives everything away so I play that to my advantage. I'm expressive when I don't need to be to throw her off my bluff. Eventually, I'm down to my bra and panties while Wrenn is completely naked on top and only has on her jeans and panties.

"I don't know if I can stop calling you Princess. It's obvious what it does to you." Wrenn smirks proudly. I hate that she knows calling me that goes right to my pussy.

"I don't know what you're talking about," I lie, crossing my arms.

"Come on." Wrenn gets on her knees and crawls over to where I'm sitting on the floor. "You can't tell me your pussy doesn't *drip* at the sound of me saying *Princess*."

I stare Wrenn down, attempting my hardest to stay strong. But fuck, I'm a weak woman. Wrenn seems to be my kryptonite.

"Fuck it." I toss the cards behind me and pull Wrenn in for a kiss.

Her lips swallow mine, our tongues fighting for control. I don't care, I want her too much to care. I give in, letting her have all the power. She bites on my bottom lip, pulls it out just a bit and lets it go. Then she grips my chin, tilts my head back and spits in my mouth. Something that I didn't know I was into before this moment. I kiss her with her hand on my neck. She squeezes in all the right places, and I groan into her mouth.

"Oh Wrenn," I moan. I know how much she loves it when I say her name.

Wrenn kisses my neck. Her teeth graze over where she's already marked me, and I whimper. It's a little more sore than I care to admit. She finds a new spot and begins sucking, hard. Her warm tongue slides down my throat. My thighs clench together. I'm sure she could tell how aroused I am.

"Is my Princess wet for me?" Wrenn dips two fingers down the front of my panties. She slips her fingers through my folds, and I whimper as she drags them to her lips and sucks them clean.

"Well?" she prompts.

"Shut up." I groan.

"Make me." She smirks.

I push her body back onto the ground and hold her chest as I climb to sit on her face. She moves my panties to the side and there's a loud ripping sound.

"Those were expensive." I growl.

"Oops," she says smugly.

I decide to shut her up by pressing my pussy to her lips. She opens her mouth and I begin grinding on her face. I hold on to the coffee table for support as I ride her face. My pussy is dripping down her tongue, down to her chin. But she continues eating me like she hasn't eaten all day. Which, thinking of it, I'm sure she didn't have any dinner.

"Mmm," she hums under me.

I gasp and slip my hand to my pussy. I swirl my fingers across my clit as she tongues me. I ride her face like an amusement park ride. She moans and I can feel my orgasm coming. The tightening of my core, the heat building, my breath becoming uneven. Suddenly I feel the urge to pee, and I know I'm about to squirt all over Wrenn's face. Only serves her right for ripping my panties.

"Fuck! Oh, god! Wrenn!" I scream out and sure enough, I burst all over Wrenn. Her tongue runs across my lips as she tries to catch all of it.

When my orgasm passes, I climb off Wrenn and sit on the other side of her. I need a second to catch my breath. But Wrenn seems to have something else on her mind. She dives between my thighs and before I can push her off, she's eating me out again. Her fingers pump in and out of me while I pant her name. She's going for *multiples*. She fucks me hard with her fingers until I'm tightening around her again.

"Fuck! Wrenn!" I scream as she makes me come.

"God, I love when you scream my name, Princess." She winks and licks her fingers clean.

"Oh, don't start." I growl.

"Someone's grumpy. Did I not satisfy you?"

"You might have." I shrug. I like being a brat with her.

"Brat. You fucking get over here if you need another." She calls me out.

Instead of answering, I crawl over to her and slide between her thighs. I run my fingers over her jeans, and she breathes heavy. I tip my head to the side, smirking at how easy it was to get a rise out of her. Slowly, I slide my hand up Wrenn's stomach. I play with the silver metal bars and watch as her nipples harden. I kiss wet, open-mouthed kisses up her stomach and around her chest. Watch as her breathing becomes labored each time I touch her breast. I can tell she's just itching for it.

"Stay still," I tell her for the third time. She keeps touching me when I'm trying to tease her.

"Make me." She smirks back.

I reach to grab her hands and hold them over her head. But the second I let go, they are back on me. Growling, I get up and ignore her calling after me. I head to my room and grab the pair of handcuffs I have sitting in the boxes for the bachelorette party. It's supposed to be a gag gift for everyone, but I can spare a pair. They are fully functional —at least for sex.

"Where did you…oh? Princess is into bondage, didn't see that coming," she muses.

"You okay with this?" I ask, holding them up as I take my position between her legs again.

"Yes, very much so." She nods.

"Good." I take her wrists, hold them together, and lock them while they're over her head. It isn't impossible to get free, but the way I had her hands, she couldn't touch me.

I go back to trailing my tongue down her center. Licking her belly button seems to be a big deal, so I watch as she moans every time. I finally tug down her jeans and toss them aside. Her cotton panties are soaked with a huge wet circle on the front. I can smell her arousal and imagine how good she'll feel on my tongue.

"Now look who's wet," I tease.

My fingers dance across her pussy and down her inner thighs. Wrenn groans, and I wonder how long it will take to break her. I could tease her all night long because Wrenn was just as stubborn as me. I bend down to kiss her inner thigh, pushing down her hips as they buck, hoping to get more. Wrenn whimpers as I lick her inner thigh to her pussy. Her panties were doing nothing at this point, so I slide them achingly slow down her legs.

"Just call me Ryleigh and I'll be happy to take care of that." I smile.

"No can do, Princess." She laughs.

"Okay."

I lean down and press my lips to her upper thigh. I bite down on the tan flesh, and she groans again. I hate and love how stubborn she is. I'm ready to tease her all night, but I press my lips to the center of her pussy just above her clit and she moans.

"Ryleigh! Okay! I know your name now, just fuck me, please!" She says begrudgingly.

When I stick my tongue against her clit, she moans my name. I lap up all the wetness she has, her sweetness dripping on my tongue. Wrenn is wrecked under me. I suck on her clit, the swollen bud begging to be touched. My fingers slide right in, and I curl them tonward me inside her.

"Oh god! Ryleigh!" Wrenn cries out and as I continue, she comes all over my hand.

"Fuck," I mutter.

I stick my fingers in her mouth and have her lick them clean. Then I kiss her, leaning over to steady myself. While kissing her,

I unhook the handcuffs and she shoves her hands into my hair again. She kisses me hard and fiercely, like she can't get enough of me. Or maybe she just doesn't want this to end. Our bodies are colliding, our hips begging to be touched. Wrenn isn't the one in control tonight. She's as needy as I was under her touch. I know I'm not going to let this night end yet.

Wrenn

"Come to the bedroom," Ryleigh mumbles against my lips.

"Yours or mine?" I ask.

"Hmm." She pauses like she's weighing the pros and cons.

"Mine," I decide. I have something in there that I want to try.

"Okay." She starts to grab the clothes, but I grab her ass.

"Leave 'em." I squeeze her ass and lean in to kiss her.

She pulls away, and we walk down the hall to my room. I shoo Cheeto out of the room and close the door, so she's not tempted to come back. Ryleigh lays in my bed with her thighs spread open. God, she has a really fucking sexy pussy. Not everyone's pussy looked and tasted like Ryleigh's. She's so fucking sweet, especially when she squirts for me.

"Can we use this?" I ask, picking up my massager wand.

"Yes." Ryleigh smiles.

I plug it in on the nightstand and look at Ryleigh.

"Come sit here." I instruct and climb behind her. She backs up into my lap and I slide my hands around the front of her.

Her pussy was still just as wet, so I turn the massager to life and press it to her pussy. Ryleigh moans under it, and I grab her boob in my free hand. Teasing Ryleigh, I turn up the speed high and then the slowest setting, going back and forth between the two. This was payback for making me say her name.

"Come on Princess. You're so wet, aren't you?" I tease in her ear.

"God yes," she moans out.

"Good girl," I whisper.

I turn up the intensity one last time, to the highest setting. Ryleigh cries out as I hold her body against mine. I move the wand over her clit, and she starts squirming under my arms. I pinch her nipple between my fingers and watch as she cries out my name.

"Oh Wrenn! Yes!" She screams. Damn, I wish I had neighbors just so they could tell us to keep it down.

I move the wand away, turning it off but keeping it on the nightstand. Ryleigh relaxes against me, and I kiss her neck softly. When her breathing calms down, she turns around and starts kissing me. We kiss like this for a while our lips lazily sliding against each other.

"Do you want some dinner?" Ryleigh asks.

"Why?"

"Because I can hear your stomach growling." She laughs. Her head is right on my belly button.

"Yeah, I forgot to have dinner," I grumble.

"Come on." Ryleigh stands up, grabs her shirt, and runs to the kitchen.

I toss on an oversized T-shirt from the closet and follow after her. She's standing with the fridge doors open, trying to decide what to make.

"We can just have cereal., I say, picking up a box of Rice Krispies.

"Or nachos?" She raises an eyebrow.

"Okay, yes please." I smile and take a seat at the counter.

"I'd ask you for help, but I'm too hungry to teach you how to use the stove."

"Hey! I'm not that bad."

"Mmm." She laughs.

Ryleigh grabs all the ingredients she needs and then turns around to start making the nachos. I'm a little too distracted looking at her bare ass as she cooks. She isn't wearing any panties so it's a nice cooking show. Whenever she stretches to get something in a high cabinet, she shows a little sliver of her wet, shiny pussy. By the time she was done cooking, I'm more turned on than hungry.

"Holy shit, this is so good." I groan.

"Be careful, those are the sounds you usually make for me," she teases.

"You both taste delicious." I shrug.

Ryleigh blushes and picks up another chip. She's standing beside me, eating with her fingers and sucking them clean each time.

"Stop looking at me like that and eat!" She playfully shoves me, and I laugh.

"Okay." I slide onto the floor under the counter and press my tongue to her pussy.

"W-what are you doing?" Ryleigh gasps.

"You said to eat!" I smirk between her legs.

Ryleigh relaxes as I hoop my arms around her thighs to steady her. As I taste her pussy, she moans for me. I'm pretty sure I still hear the crunch of chips like she's eating. But after a moan where she almost chokes, I don't hear another chip after that. I grab her ass, pushing her pussy closer in my face.

"Yes!" she cries out, and I can tell she's close.

So I stand up, wipe my mouth clean and pop a nacho in my mouth. Ryleigh looks at me with the look of pure shock on her face. I smirk as I continue eating and Ryleigh readjusts herself. She goes back to eating too, while squeezing her thighs together and shooting me evil looks.

"You're so going to pay for that," she mumbles as we clean up our food.

"Oh yeah?" I laugh.

"I bet I'll have you begging on your knees before me."

"Ha! I think we already proved today I can last longer than you."

"Ugh, whatever." She groans.

"We could, uh, go be adventurous with my toy collection." I shrug.

"Do you have a strap on?" Ryleigh asks with glimmering eyes.

"Yes." I smile.

"Go put it on, and I'll meet you in the bedroom."

I fight the urge to tell her not to tell me what to do. But she's commanding the room at the moment, and I'm here for it. So I disappear into the bedroom, grab the box of adult toys from the back of my closet, and grab the strap on. It's black, 8.5 inches long, and thick as hell. Sometimes when I wear it, it makes me feel invincible. Like, if I had a real dick, it'd be this big and everyone would be jealous.

So when Ryleigh returns in a pink laced bodysuit and poses in my doorway, I drop to my knees. I crawl over to where Ryleigh stands, and she smirks as she looks down at me. I don't know how she did it, but somehow, I'm weak when it comes to her. She spreads her thighs, and I can see her dripping down her inner thigh. I move forward and wait for her to say yes.

She nods and I press my tongue to her pussy. Licking her through the lace, I was driving her crazy. Reaching between us, I pop open the buttons and the lace swings forward. Perfect access to her pussy now. I lick her clit, sucking gently on the swollen bud. Then I slip two fingers in her pussy and look up as she moans and pushes my head closer to her. Before she gets any closer, I pull away and stand up. I grab her by the hips, lead her to my dresser and set her hands on the top of it. Grabbing her hips, I pull her toward me, ass in the air. I run the dildo across her pussy before sliding it in slowly. I wanted to be sure she could take it all.

"You got it Princess, you can do this," I coax in her ear.

She leans into me, letting me slide in completely. Ryleigh moans, and I wait for her to adjust before I move. But she backs her hips into mine, and I take that as a sign to move. I hold her hips and start bucking my hips into hers. Ryleigh screams out with each thrust.

"Oh, Wrenn!" she cries out before slumping over the dresser while I slide out of her.

The entire dildo is soaked with her juices. I walk to my night-stand and grab a tissue to wipe it off for now. Ryleigh follows me over to the bed and slips the harness off me.

"What if I want to wear it?" she asks, biting her lip.

"You can definitely wear it, Princess." I pick it up off the nightstand and hand it to Ryleigh.

She puts it on, and fuck if I'm not already turned on. Ryleigh looks hot as fuck and ready to take control. She points at the bed, and I lie down, waiting for her to tell me what to do.

"I want you on top," she decides.

I nod. Letting her lay down, I slide on top of her hips. Positioning myself over the strap on, I slide down slowly and moan.

"Damn, I like you on top." Ryleigh groans.

I put my hands on her chest, grabbing each breast. Then I bounce up and down on her lap. The toy slides in and out of me, just so. My hair flies all around as I move faster and faster. I'm horny and my knees can only bounce for so long. Ryleigh looks up at me, touching my tits and playing with my nipples.

"Fuck me. Oh, god!" I cry out.

Ryleigh leans in to kiss me. Her lips cover my cries with each movement. I let one hand go and bounce. The friction of the toy and Ryleigh's thighs were too much for me. I'm too fucking close.

"Come for me," Ryleigh says, gripping my chin.

Her words send me over the edge, whimpering her name. My legs feel like jelly, so I slide off Ryleigh and lie on the other side of the bed. My head hits the pillows, and I'm instantly tired.

Ryleigh excuses herself to clean up, and I watch her ass move as she goes.

"Here, I brought you some water." Ryleigh hands me a glass and I sit up to drink it.

"Thanks." I hand her the empty glass and she places it on the nightstand.

Ryleigh climbs into bed next to me, and I'm afraid she's going to talk about us. Instead, she's quiet as she runs her fingers through my hair. She twirls one piece for a while and then twists it another way. Her fingertips are soft when they touch the side of my face. It's the first time I've been around her and I actually feel calm. Everything around us is quiet for once.

I lean in to kiss her, and her lips softly caress mine. I pull her body into mine, and I get lost in her lips. My hands sink in her hair as hers slip into mine. Holding each other, our lips do all the communicating. I wanted to live in her taste.

I ignore the nagging sense of feeling this happy with some-one. I know what this is, and I don't even want to think about it. I know better, nothing is happening here. So I need to get out of this quick. Or at least try to distance myself from her. Maybe starting tomorrow? She kisses me again. Okay, maybe the next day? Why did being with her have to feel so good?

We are so hot together we could probably literally start a fire. As much as I want to keep sleeping with her, it's well out of revenge territory at this point. I need to be the one to end this thing, and I can't do that if she beats me to it. Tomorrow I'll try to sneak out before her again. Hopefully my sister won't be coming over and I could wake up early.

Ryleigh lets out a deep moan, and I press my lips to hers one last time. She sinks into my arms, and I ignore how nice this feels. No. I'm not going to let this woman break my heart, again. Even if she didn't know she did the first time. I'm stronger and wiser than I was before. I can't hand her the chance to hurt me again. Ryleigh falls asleep in my arms, and I pull her close to me.

Whatever happens, at least we have tonight. I stare down at her while she sleeps, willing myself to keep hating her. I can't let go of the past that easily, can I?

SEVENTEEN

Ryleigh

I wake up in Wrenn's arms. Her body is pulled tight against mine, her arms wrapped around my stomach. Was Wrenn actually cuddling me? I didn't know that was even something she knew how to do. If she found us like this, I'm sure she'd find some way to blame me.

I move a little just to stretch, and Wrenn groans. I place her arm by her side and climb out of bed. I'm naked but I really have to pee. So I scurry to Wrenn's bathroom, close the door behind me, and pee. I'm washing my hands when I look at my neck. She added a few new spots. I'll have to remember to cover those up if I go out.

I slip back into bed, and Wrenn opens her eyes, yawning at me.

"Good morning." I smile.

"Morning." She groans.

"I never would've pegged you for a cuddler," I tease.

"Ugh, I thought you were a pillow," she lies.

Wrenn's eyes are closed, but I look at her and smile. I hate that she is making me feel this way and she doesn't even know it. I know better than to fall for my best friend's little sister, but I guess I don't know enough to not sleep with her. This is the second time we've been in bed together this week. Yet, with no chance of being caught this morning, it begs the question. What are we?

"Wrenn?" I say softly.

"Yes?" She opens one eye and looks at me.

"We should talk."

"No, we shouldn't," she grumbles and closes her eyes tightly.

"Wrenn…"

"No. I'm not fucking doing this. Not again." She jumps out of bed, realizes she's naked, and starts looking for new clothes.

"Come on, I just want to talk about this."

"I don't want to." She throws her arms in the air and tosses a shirt over her head.

"I can't fucking do this again, Ryleigh. I don't know what you want to freaking talk about." She steps angrily into her shorts.

"I just think we should talk about this." I stand up and follow her as she walks out of the room.

"Because you did such a good job of that last time?" Wrenn says, stopping me in my tracks. She's never brought that up before. I didn't know if she even remembered what happened. But of course, she did.

"I-I want this time to be different," I admit.

"Not interested." Wrenn shrugs.

She starts the coffee maker and grabs a mug.

"Aren't you the least bit curious to discuss whatever's going on with us?" I ask.

"I'm more interested in knowing if you wanna have sex." Wrenn turns around, and my jaw drops.

"What?"

"Drop this conversation, and I'll eat you out on this counter before I've even had my coffee," Wrenn proposes, patting the empty counter.

"Why can't we do both?"

"Nope. Limited time offer." Wrenn taps her wrist like an imaginary watch is there.

"You are so infuriating," I grumble, walking over to her.

"Pretty sure that's what you love about me, Princess." She laughs as I sit on the counter.

"We will have the conversation…*eventually*." I lose all sense of thought when she puts her tongue on my clit.

My vision goes blurry as she eats me out. I'm completely naked, playing with my nipples. Wrenn is between my thighs, at the perfect height. The way she touches me makes me want to light something on fire. She makes me equally angry and turned on. How am I ever going to get her to talk to me and clear the air if all we do is have sex?

Maybe that's the solution I didn't realize. If all Wrenn wants to do is hookup, then maybe they're both on the same page. It isn't like I'm looking for something serious. I just want to make sure I don't hurt her this time. So we are probably fine. We'd be like friends with benefits ,without the friends part. Enemies with benefits.

Wrenn sucks hard on my clit and I come, screaming. "Holy shit!" I yell as I hop off the counter.

"Careful there, don't wanna break anything, Princess."

"I'm fine," I insist and stand up fully even though I do feel a little lightheaded.

"Go get dressed, I can't focus when you're naked."

"Good to know, maybe I should ditch my clothes for good," I tease.

"Fine by me. But only if I'm allowed to go naked too."

I shake my head and walk to the bedroom. I pass the art room and realize it's been a few days since I've painted or done any kind of art. I get the sudden urge to draw something. So I put some clothes on, walk to the art room, and sit at my easel. I grab my pencil. I want to make sure I get this right, so that might include a few sketches of the outline. Once it finally looks good enough to start, I decide to grab my paints.

"Where'd you go?" Wrenn asks as I come back in the kitchen. An empty bowl of cereal and a spoon is sitting next to her.

"I got inspired. I'm gonna paint for a bit." I grab my brushes from the sink and a glass of water.

"Okay, but don't ask me to model for you again. I *just* got all that paint out of my hair," Wrenn teases.

I laugh and head back to the room. The lighting is perfect this time of day, and I want to start it now before I lose my momentum. I make my pallet and start. Relaxing into the painting, I calm down a bit. Wrenn has a tendency to rile me up, and my painting was a way of negating that. With each stroke, I felt lighter and more relaxed.

I'm taking a second to stretch when Wrenn saunters through the art room in nothing but a towel over her shoulder. My jaw drops as I check out her ass. She makes sure to turn around at the last second and wink at me. I guess she's doing her morning laps. At least she'll be in a better mood. She always seems to be more relaxed after she swims every morning.

I try to focus on the painting, but it's hard when every so often I see Wrenn's ass pop out of the water. Or her breasts sitting perfectly on her chest as she walked around the pool. It's like she's trying to drive me crazy. I slide myself off the stool and stand to do my painting. But she's getting in my head again. I put on my headphones, and with the help of my favorite band, the Jonas Brothers, I'm about to tune her out.

I'm done with the first layer by the time Wrenn comes inside for lunch. I don't know if she has work again today, but she should be able to drive herself if she does. Last night, hanging out with her at work was fun. I had just wanted to keep an eye on her while she sobered up, but to my surprise, she kept talking to me most of the night. She originally told me not to talk to her, and then she was the one hanging out with me. I think she likes hanging out with me more than she cares to admit.

"You still working?" Wrenn drips on the hardwood floor.

"Nope, just finishing up," I say, picking up the cup of water and dirty brushes.

"I have work in two hours so I'm gonna grab a shower... unless you wanna join me?" She wiggles a brow.

"I actually need some food. I'm starving. Raincheck?" I smile.

"Sure."

I think she's surprised I turned down the shower, but she doesn't let on. That is something about Wrenn, when it comes to me, she keeps how she feels close to the belt. I make a smoothie and some avocado toast for breakfast. I need to replenish my energy after all the sex we had last night. While Wrenn's in the shower, I decide to head to my room and call Kim.

"Hey! What's going on?" she answers the phone cheerfully.

"I had sex with Wrenn!" I squeal quietly.

"Again?"

"I mean yeah, last night."

"Last night? I thought you meant the other day when you tried hiding those hickies on your neck."

"Well, it was sort of both," I admit.

"Oh my god. I need to sit down." Kim groans.

"Come on, it's not that bad."

"Alana might have the world's biggest freakout. She seems like she's hanging on by a thread right now."

"It's not like anyone has to *tell* her."

"Did you guys at least talk this time?"

"Well, I tried. But she ate me out on the counter instead, and I think that was way more fun."

"Oh god, remind me not to eat at your house anymore." Kim makes a gagging sound.

"You might wanna stay out of the living room too then." I giggle.

"Did you just call to brag about where you did it?"

"No, I actually called because I wasn't sure what I should do. I've tried talking to her a lot and she just doesn't want to hear it. She completely cuts off the conversation before it starts."

"I mean, you can't force someone to talk to you….but it does make for a messy situation if you both aren't clear about what it is."

"I know, you're right." I sigh.

"I guess, keep trying when you can. Maybe try to hold off sleeping with her again if you can."

"You make it sound like I'm a sex addict." I fake scoff.

"Not at all. But there is something about Wrenn that seems to *rile* you up."

"She just gets under my skin," I grumble.

"Exactly, but from what I saw the other day? There was a lot of chemistry between you guys too."

"Really?"

"Oh yes. But I'd be careful because I think Alana was picking up on that too."

"Got it." I swallow hard.

"Let me go, I'm about to cook lunch. Good luck, okay?"

"Thanks. Enjoy lunch."

I hang up feeling more confused than before. Did Wrenn and I really have chemistry? Like, more chemistry than just sex and no emotions? Did it matter? I couldn't imagine a world where Alana would be okay with us being together. Or a world where Wrenn actually talked to me like a grown up about what we were doing. I was the older one here, sure just by four years. But maybe it was time to realize that Wrenn was too immature for me, and it will only ever be sex between us.

Groaning, I fall back into my bed, and an orange ball meows at me.

"I'm sorry Cheeto, I didn't see ya there." I let her smell my hand before I attempt to pet her.

She seems to be okay with me, so I pet behind her ears, and she purrs. Why can't humans be this simple? Nothing to talk about, just if you want me to touch you, purr lightly. Scratch me if it's no. Cheeto rubs her head against my hand and turns over to show me her belly. I pet gently. We are still getting to know each other, but it seems like she likes me.

Wrenn's shower stops, and I think about her perfect, wet body stepping out of the tub. She's probably standing in her room, dripping wet hair on the carpet, while she looks for something to wear to work. Her body glistening with water as she towel dries off. I wish I had said yes to that shower. But I know I'll be painting the rest of the day and there is no point. Besides, all the sex has made my pussy sore. I might need to sit on ice for at least the rest of the day to relax it.

EIGHTEEN

Ryleigh

Gemma texts me asking if I can come over because planning a bachelorette party over text is just not it. So before Wrenn wakes up, I drive over to Norah and Gemma's place on the Estate. Norah opens the door with a smile. Her red hair is tied back in a bun today, and she's wearing a loose sundress. I'm holding too many boxes to give her a hug.

"Come on in, Gemma's in the dining room trying to organize everything she bought." She leads me toward the back, and I plop the boxes on the only empty spot on the floor.

"I might have gone overboard," Gemma admits. She's a bit taller than me, her body fuller, and she's wearing a pair of hospital scrubs. I think Alana mentioned she was one of those traveling nurses.

"I'm Ryleigh by the way." I smile and go for a hug. She's one of Alana's best friends which means she was one of us.

"Gemma." Her dark brown hair is in a messy ponytail with a pen sticking out the top.

"So, what are you thinking?"

Norah leaves us alone to plan. Gemma has a lot of the games and decorations planned out, but what she doesn't have is a guest list or a venue. I offer up Teddys, considering it's close by, and Wrenn might be able to convince the owners to give it to us for cheap. I show her all the sex toy gifts I got for the gift bags ,and she laughs along with me. Norah's sitting on the couch in the room behind us, reading a book on her Kindle.

"Is that the same one you've always had?" I ask Norah.

"Yes, it still works." She holds up her Kindle that has to be at least a decade old. She loves it and refuses to turn it in for a new one.

"She's had that thing since high school," I whisper to Gemma.

"I heard that! You know I prefer a real book anyway," Norah points out.

She has always been a book lover, it was no different now. I don't remember a time when I saw Norah without a book nearby. She even worked at the local bookstore, To Be Loved. I had a feeling it was in attempt to save some money from all the books she buys.

"Do you read?" Gemma asks.

"Not really. I read Britney Spears' biography, but that's the extent of it," I admit. "What about you?"

"I read a lot at work during my down time. But I have a pretty recent Kindle, because it's not as heavy to carry around."

"That makes sense."

"Do you guys want lunch?" Norah asks.

"I'm okay."

"I think there's some leftover lasagna from last night if you want," Gemma says to Norah.

But the second she does, Norah's face turns green, and she covers her mouth. Running to what I assume is the bathroom, she slams the door shut behind her. Gemma runs after her, stopping to grab something in the kitchen before she disappears in the bathroom with Norah. Was she okay? What the hell just happened?

Two flushes and fifteen minutes later, they both emerge from the bathroom. I give them a curious look.

"Are you okay?" I look at Norah.

"There's something I have to tell you," Norah says quietly.

"You're scaring me, dude. What's going on?"

Norah takes a seat on the couch, and I sit next to her, waiting for whatever she has to tell me.

"I'm pregnant," she starts. I'm immediately excited, knowing this is something she's wanted for a while. But then I'm confused about the logistics of it.

"Let me explain." She pauses. "When Finn passed, we were in the process of attempting IVF. We weren't going to mention it to anyone until we were sure it worked. I was actually at the doctor when I got the call that he was in an accident. We stopped the procedure and put the embryos on ice. I figured I'd wait until he was better, and we'd try again. But obviously that didn't happen, so I decided recently that I want to be a mom. And I wasn't looking to be in a relationship again, so I thought I'd use my and Finn's embryos and get pregnant. Well, I did IVF, and now I'm pregnant."

"Wow." The words slip off my tongue. "Okay, so how are you feeling?"

"Wait, that's it?" She looks surprised at my response.

"You've always wanted to be a mom. I don't see why I should be surprised. I'm happy you found a way to do it and honor Finn. He would've been a great dad." I grab her hand and squeeze it.

"I wish he was here." She starts to cry. I'm about to offer her a hug when Gemma takes my place. She sits on the other side of her, and Norah falls on her shoulder, letting out all her tears. It's obvious now that there is something going on between them.

"Do you need some tea? That usually helps," Gemma says quietly.

"Yes please." Norah nods.

Gemma disappears into the kitchen, and I shoot Norah a look. She blushes the color of her hair and smiles.

"So, when did that start?" I wink.

"I don't know. It's sort of new."

"Now that's something I didn't see coming," I admit. For all the years I've known Norah, she's only been with men. Granted, for most of our lives it was one man, but still. It's weird to imagine her with anyone but Finn. But to find out it's a woman? Definitely not on my bingo card.

"I didn't either. She makes me *happy*." Norah smiles softly.

"Then I'm happy for you, and your secret is safe with me." I hold her hand tightly.

"Here you are." Gemma hands her a cup of hot tea and sits back down next to her.

"I'll eventually tell everyone. But with the wedding and it being so early…"

"I understand. Mums the word." I nod.

"Why don't we finish up the bachelorette party plans so Norah can rest?" Gemma asks, looking at me.

"Sure," I agree. I like how she seems to take care of Norah. It's nice to see someone looking out for her again.

"If she needs anything baby related or not, you call me, okay? I'll be right there," I tell Gemma quietly.

"I understand. I'm glad she told you. I think only Heather knows."

"Gotcha."

"So, do you have the number of a local stripper?" Gemma asks.

"I do, we actually went to high school with him, I think." I grimace. It was a small town; it wasn't like there were a ton of options when it came to strippers here.

"Is that okay?" Gemma raises an eyebrow.

"Well, yeah? I mean, it doesn't do anything for me, but it'll be funny to watch Alana freak out." I laugh.

"She will definitely freak out. She tried to make me promise no strippers, but of course I never agreed."

"Hey Gem?" Norah calls from the couch.

Gemma rushes to her side. I can't hear what they're talking

about, but I can see the way they look at each other. Maybe Norah isn't sure of how they feel, but it's obvious to me. Gemma is smitten with her, just as much as Norah is with her. Gemma touches her forehead, probably checking for a fever, and Norah looks into her eyes. They speak quietly, and Gemma disappears into the kitchen. She returns a few minutes later with a sleeve of crackers and some water. Norah gives her a soft smile that lights Gemma up like a Christmas tree.

Part of me wishes I could have something like that. Where someone just smiled about having me around and took care of me when I was sick. I had Wrenn, but in reality, I didn't really *have* her. She and I had sex and we flirted, but we also fought and never agreed on anything important. I mean, she wouldn't even talk to me about what the hell was going on between us. That couldn't be the start of a good relationship. Or any kind of relationship. But when I look at her, I knew I feel similar to the way Gemma and Norah feel about each other.

"Hey, I'm gonna take off," I say, looking at the clock. It was later than I thought, and I wanted to get out of their hair.

"You sure?" Norah asks.

"Yeah, I think we have everything. I'll call the stripper tomorrow and finalize the date," I tell Gemma.

"Awesome, then I'll send out the E-invites." We had decided after stuffing five hundred envelopes for the wedding that it would be much simpler to send out email invitations for the bachelorette.

"Bye Norah, take care." I hug my oldest friend and head out the door.

When I get home, I don't see Wrenn's car in the driveway. She must still be at work. I make myself dinner, grab dinner for Cheeto and watch a movie on the couch alone. I'm pretty bored and exhausted by the time the movie is over, so I decide to head to bed.

I lie in my clothes, too lazy to put on my pajamas yet. Too lazy to even get under the sheets. My brain is just thinking about

Wrenn and what is going on between us. I hate that I care. I hate that I'm starting to have real feelings for someone who was so infuriating. But really, I'm just mad that I am the reason she doesn't want to talk. I ghosted her last time ,so of course she doesn't want to bother bringing that up.

I thought she was just trying to seduce me, but every time we sleep together it happens again. Was she just content hooking up with me now? Is that all we'd ever be? I'm not sure if I'm okay with that. Besides running the risk of Alana finding out the longer it goes on, I don't know if I can emotionally handle that. Ugh, why can't it just be simpler? I'm about to scream into my pillow when I hear a knock at my door.

"Hello?" I sit up and wait for a reply. It has to be Wrenn, right?

"Hey." Wrenn's voice carries through the door.

"What's going on?" I open the door and look at her, confused.

"Wanna go for a drive?"

"Right now?" I glance out the window. It's dark already and definitely past midnight if Wrenn is already home from work.

"Yeah." She shrugs, her hands in the front pockets of her jeans.

"Where?"

"I don't know. Are you coming or not?" She looks impatient.

"Okay, okay. Hold on." I grab my cardigan off my chair. It's chilly tonight and I don't want to be cold.

I follow Wrenn to her car and slide in the passenger side. I expect her to put on the GPS or something to give me a clue to where we're going. But she doesn't even touch her phone. She pulls out of the driveway and starts heading toward town. All the places in town are already closed so it isn't like she can be taking us anywhere there.

"There's no destination, Princess. Haven't you ever been on a drive just for the hell of it?" She smirks at me.

"Of course, but not in Lovers," I admit. There isn't much to do or see just driving around our small town.

She laughs but doesn't say anything. I start to relax, looking out the front window and waiting to see something familiar. Wrenn is quiet as she drives. There's no music playing or anything but the sound of the tires on the old roads. Maybe this is something I could get used to.

NINETEEN

Wrenn

Ryleigh is quieter than normal, but I guess that's what happens when I've been avoiding talking to her all week. I don't know what came over me, but when I got home from work, I saw her bedroom light was still on. Part of me wanted to ask her to hookup, but the other part of me just wanted to hang out with her. I didn't see her today since she was gone before breakfast. I spent most of my day at work thinking about her. What the hell was up with that? So I decided to take her on a late night drive with me. It's what I usually did when I needed to clear my head.

"Here, you can put on some music." I hand her the aux cord and she smiles.

"Thanks." She fishes her phone out of her pocket and starts scrolling on Spotify.

An unfamiliar song comes blaring through the speakers. It takes me a moment before I realize I actually do know the song.

"Are you seriously playing the Jonas Brothers right now?" I scoff.

"I don't know if I'm offended you don't like them or impressed you know who they are." She laughs.

"I'm not that much younger than you," I remind her.

"True." She nods. The 'Year 3000' plays in the background while I drive.

"What were you up to today?" I ask casually.

"I was with Norah and Gemma, planning the bachelorette party."

"Did you book the stripper?" I laugh.

"Not yet, I have to call tomorrow." She blushes.

"If you need someone more experienced, I'd be happy to call."

"Oh please, I'm plenty experienced thank you." She rolls her eyes.

"Whatever you say, Princess."

The song changes to another Jonas Brothers song and I laugh. Of course, this girl would be blaring them as we take a midnight drive. Somehow Ryleigh still manages to surprise me.

"What do you think of Will?" she asks.

"My sister's fiancé?" I glance at her ,and she nods. "He's fine I guess."

"Hmm."

"Why?"

"There's something off about Alana and the wedding."

"She's just stressed." I shrug.

"No, it's more than that. I've seen Norah in wedding planning mode and she and her fiancé were more in love than ever. Alana seems to be on edge, and I haven't seen Will once all summer."

"You're not missing much."

"What do you mean?" she asks.

"I've seen him a few times at family dinners and he's kind of boring. He's always on his phone and doesn't say too much to anyone." I shrug.

"But Alana seems happy when she's with him?"

"I-I don't know," I admit.

Now that I think about it, I've never seen her *happy* with a guy she's brought home. She seems content enough, they date for a few years and then a breakup always happened. Will is the first one she brought home that actually is sticking it out for the long term. Which sort of surprised me. She's not *unhappy* with him. But I can't say she looks like she's head over heels for him either. Maybe she just isn't that kind of person when she falls in love. I've never been like that either.

"I just worry they're rushing into this." She sighs.

"It's Alana's life. I'm not getting in the middle of anything," I say firmly. My mother would kill me if I had a hand in undoing Alana's marriage.

"Okay." Ryleigh slumps in her seat.

"Wanna see some stars?" I ask as we drive toward the lighthouse.

"Right now?"

"Duh." I laugh.

"Okay." She smiles.

I park the car close to the dock, then lead her down the chained off path. She hesitates for a second, but when I offer her my hand she seems to relax. I'm not the biggest fan of holding hands but Ryleigh's hand seemed to fit with mine. I walk along the deck, and we sit on the edge.

"Look, there's the North Star." I point, looking up.

"Really?"

"Honestly I have no idea," I admit.

"You bring a lot of girls up here?" she asks.

"Nope, you might be the first, Princess." I wink.

"It's nice out here."

"I usually take a drive out here when I need to think."

"What are you thinking about tonight?"

"Life." I frown. I wish I could be more specific with her, but I'm not willing to wear my heart on my sleeve. Oh no, that shit is locked up with a key.

"Anything in particular?"

"Not really, just a lot going on lately."

Ryleigh's quiet, and I can tell what she's thinking about. I know she's been trying to talk about 'us' but I still didn't know what that even means.

"Sometimes I wish I could live off my paintings."

"Why can't you?" I ask.

"I'd need to sell them for a lot more if I wanted to make a career of it. I think it's probably time I get serious about my life and look for a *real* job." She sighs.

"You can't be serious."

"What?"

"You're so freaking talented. You can't stop making art just because it's not a 'real' job. If it's a job and you're getting paid, then why isn't it real? Because it's a creative field? I'd kill to have as much talent as you do."

"Did you go to school?"

"I did. I'm about a semester short of graduating. But I hated the path I was on, so I dropped out. Became the family disappointment you see before you."

"That's not true," Ryleigh says softly.

"My mother would disagree." I scoff. Ryleigh reaches for my hand and entangles her fingers with mine.

"What did you go to school for?"

"Business," I grumble.

"Do you enjoy business? Isn't that a lot of math?"

"Yes, and no I hated it. But my parents encouraged me to go for something practical."

"What did you want to go for?"

"It's stupid."

"Tell me. Please?" Ryleigh smiles and I sigh.

"I wanted to be a journalist."

"That's not stupid."

"Really?" I snap my head up to look at her.

"Yeah, I mean you'd be a great journalist. You have a great poker face and always know the gossip in town."

"I think it requires a little more than that." I laugh.

"I think if it's what you want to do then you should go for it.

Your parents might want you to do something, but I don't see when you've ever not been true to yourself."

"Thanks," I mumble. I didn't intend to get so deep about myself with Ryleigh. But it's simple with her. When we aren't fighting or having sex.

"Do you think you'd go back to school for it or is that like, a job where you could just jump right in?" she asks.

"Honestly, I'm not sure. Considering the job market today I'd assume I need some kind of a degree."

"If it's something you want then you shouldn't be afraid to go for it."

"I'll go for it if you keep making your art," I decide.

"That's a tough deal, but fair." Ryleigh nods.

Sitting in silence, we watch the water for a bit. The sky is so dark that at the edge of the water it melts into the sky. If not for the stars illuminating the night, you couldn't see where the edge was. I kick my feet over the dock and Ryleigh's hand is still holding mine. My stomach feels like it's filled with butterflies. What the hell was going on? Was I really having feelings right now? If I could vomit them up, I would. This is not the time for me to be thinking romantically about Ryleigh.

Sure, we were under the stars, but it's nighttime. I'm not trying to seduce her. I'm just... hanging out with her. Oh god, like a date. I've accidentally taken Ryleigh out on a date without realizing it. I spent most of the day thinking about her and I didn't even consider that she might think this was a date. And the award for the biggest idiot goes to. I know better than this. I know not to let feelings get involved when I'm dealing with Ryleigh. She's older and I don't think I've ever seen her in a rela-tionship. Not to mention, I was even worse at them. My last serious relationship was with Shelly in high school.

Ryleigh starts scratching her leg. Only she doesn't stop and keeps going, scratching up her leg, on her arm and even on her hand.

"What's going on? You allergic to something?"

"I think it's the mosquitos." She groans.

"Shit, come on." I stand and pull her toward me.

We run back to the car and she's still itching on the way home. The Jonas Brothers are still playing but this time I start to hum along.

"Ah hah! You do like them!" she exclaims.

"So I like one song, sue me."

"I saw you earlier too, bopping your head," she says smugly.

"Oh whatever." I roll my eyes.

"Admit you like the Jonas brothers!" She squeals.

"No way, Princess."

"Come on." She pushes out her bottom lip and opens her eyes.

"The puppy dog face doesn't work on me, sweetheart."

"Sweetheart? That's a new one."

"It felt right." I shrug.

"You're so annoying sometimes," she grumbles.

"Yet you still like me," I tease.

Ryleigh stays quiet and I know I've gotten under her skin. Her nose wrinkles and her eyebrows come together in the middle. A telltale sign that she's pissed at me. I loved how hot she looks. I also know that if I reached over and feel her panties, she'll be wet for me. Something I could guarantee. I think us fighting turns her on just as much as it turns me on.

"What are you smiling about?"

"You're just hot when you're all grumpy." I laugh.

"I'm not."

"Okay, whatever you say, Princess."

"Didn't we put a stop to that when I beat your ass in strip poker?"

"Excuse me?" I look at her. "I think you forfeited to have sex with me. I don't recall you winning."

"You can't be serious! I was in the lead!"

"So? You gave it all up to give it up to me," I say proudly.

"You're infuriating."

"Wanna pull over and jump in the back seat?" I joke.

"Wrenn!" Her cheeks darken under the moonlight.

"Ryleigh," I mimic.

Ryleigh crosses her arms over her chest as I drive. I'm still not sure where we're going. I crossed the outside of town already so I suppose I can head back. But I like it here with her. I hum along to the song where that brother says "red dress." Ryleigh stares straight ahead, but damn if I'm not in the mood to kiss her. Just knowing I can get such a rise out of her really gets me going. It's like playing with fire, and I want to see how long we can burn.

"Do you wanna go home?"

"Where else would we go?"

"I don't know. It's not like we have a lot of options here." I sigh.

"When I was in Spain, I stayed out until six a.m. dancing one night."

"I've always wanted to travel, but I never made the time."

"You should. Living in Europe was the best time of my life."

"Then why come home?"

"Everyone settles down eventually. I'll travel more again in the future." She shrugs.

"Where haven't you been that you want to go?"

"Australia for sure. I'm dying to hold a baby koala."

"They let you do that?"

"Yeah! But not like wild ones, just in the zoos."

"Shit, that's actually kind of cool," I admit.

Checking out my gas tank, I realize I should probably head for home. I'm not going to run out or anything, but I also don't want to refill it if I don't have to. I turn the car around and head straight on the path back to the Lover's Estate. Ryleigh is singing along quietly to the music, and I smile. I want to tease her but I'm afraid if I do, she might stop singing. So I don't say anything and quietly admire her from the side.

TWENTY

Ryleigh

Wrenn pulls into the driveway, and I unplug my phone from the aux cord. For some reason this feels like the end of a date. I don't know why, it's not like Wrenn and I did anything but talk tonight. But maybe that was why. For the first time all summer it was about more than just sex with us. I was open and honest with her about my art, and she opened up about school. We connected in new ways. Which is also why I don't want this night to end. I know I'm falling for her and I know that I shouldn't, but I can't help it either.

"We should, uh, go in," Wrenn says quietly.

"Sure." I nod.

I have the key so I unlock the front door and kick off my shoes. Thankfully my body isn't itchy from the mosquito bites anymore. But I'm sure the itchiness will return at some point. Wrenn is right behind me, taking off her sneakers. I'm about to say goodnight when Wrenn pulls me in by the waist and looks at me. Her dark eyes bore into mine, and I suck in a breath. Suddenly I'm nervous.

Wrenn places a hand on my neck, and I lean in. She closes her eyes and our lips touch. It's softer than how she usually kisses

145

me. With more purpose and intimacy. I can feel her hand gripping the loop of my jeans, her other hand still on my cheek. I run my fingers through her hair and rest them on her neck. Her tongue delicately slides across my lips before meeting mine. Our bodies move together, needing more of the other. But it isn't like usual. She isn't rushing to get me undressed or pulling my body to hers in a frenzy. For once, she's taking time to just kiss me. Which leaves me feeling unsteady.

"Goodnight." She smiles, pulling away.

Before I can gather my thoughts, she's down the hall in her room. What the hell just happened? I bring my hand to my lips and touch them. That kiss was *real*. That kiss was *different* than anything we've done before. But what the hell does it mean?

I walk to my bedroom and start getting ready for bed. Grabbing my pajamas, I carry them to the bathroom. I'm still thinking about the kiss while I wash my face, brush my teeth, and get undressed. Everything feels different tonight. How am I supposed to just go to bed like nothing has happened?

I climb into bed and stare at the ceiling. There's no way I'm going to be able to sleep right now. That kiss had jolted me awake. Sure, it was soft and slow, but the passion I felt behind her lips was *electric*. Did she feel that too? Is that why she ran away so quickly? I know Wrenn is afraid of us, of what things could mean if we actually talked about it. That much is clear. I've given up trying to convince her to talk to me. She'll come around when she's ready. And if she doesn't, well then that is my answer.

I just wish I didn't like her so much. If I had any say in it, I would've just let it be sex between friends. That way no one would get hurt and we could have fun. But my heart had to get involved and now I didn't know what to do. There was nothing I could do. I just hate being in this limbo. Hate giving her all this control over me.

Wrenn is beautiful and funny, and god, she has a mouth on her that is my downfall. No matter what comes out of it, she manages to make me smile. Talking to her tonight felt like the night of the wedding. We had been drinking, snuck off with a fresh bottle of champagne that I swiped from an unsuspecting waiter. Wrenn and I left the reception hall and ran about the hotel, drinking chugs straight from the bottle. We were about to sneak into the pool after hours when the hotel security guard almost caught us. We ended up kissing in the elevator to keep him off our trail. No one was going to question two people passionately making out.

What I hadn't anticipated was how good it would feel to be with her. Her kiss awakened something deep in me. But it also scared the crap out of me, so I left before she woke. I thought it would be easier that way. That if I just pretended it didn't happen, then maybe I could forget about how it made me feel. But of course, that didn't work. I left for Europe a month later and I didn't anticipate Alana's wedding to be the thing that brought me back to Lovers. Especially under the same roof as her.

Maybe I just need to be the one to break the ice. If I tell Wrenn how I'm feeling, she won't be as afraid to tell me how she feels. I need to be vulnerable with her if I ever expect her to be vulnerable with me. Even if she doesn't feel the same way, I can get over this stupid little crush and move on. It's not like I am in love with her or something.

I sit up in bed, deciding I need to talk to her now. I'm never going to sleep if I don't know where we stand. Kicking my legs off the bed, I walk to the door and open it. I almost have a heart attack when I find Wrenn on the other side with her hand raised as if she is about to knock.

"What are you doing…"

"I needed to talk to you," she says shyly.

"What about?"

"As much as I hate it, I think I'm falling for you." Wrenn looks up at me and my mouth curves into a smile.

"I hate it, but I think I am too," I admit.

I tip her chin and kiss her. Her soft lips melt into mine and just like earlier, she's softer with her kiss. She presses her body against mine and I grab her by the waist, holding her steady against me. I don't know how long we kiss. I just know that I never want to stop. Her tongue slips in my mouth, and I lightly moan as she takes a swipe across my lips before dipping back in. I feel weak in the knees. Is this what it is supposed to be like?

My arms wrap around her neck, and she scoops me up into the air. Carrying me over to the bed, she lays me down on the pillows. Climbing on top of me, she keeps kissing me, taking the time to kiss my neck, *gently*. Her hand slides up my cotton T-shirt and I gasp at her cool touch.

"Sorry, my hands are cold," she mutters against me.

"It's okay." I gasp when they reach my breasts. My nipples harden under her touch, and she plays with them carefully.

She's taking time with my body like she never has before. It's like she's getting to know it all over again. Which is making me even more turned on than usual. My breath hitches as her knee slips between my thighs against my wet core.

"Tell me you want this." She presses her head against my forehead and waits for me to respond.

"I want this."

"Tell me you want *me*." She looks deep in my eyes, searching for my response.

"I want *you*," I admit. Her lips press against mine in a moment of passion.

She climbs off me, throws her shirt off over her head in one swoop. She's wearing this black lace bra with a little pink bow on the front. I wanna know if she put it on for me or that's just what she was wearing. But she lifts my hips and slides off my shorts and panties, distracting me. Wrenn slips between my legs and starts kissing my inner thighs. Works her way up from just above my kneecap all the way to my pussy. She kisses me slowly, delicately, *purposefully*.

"P-Please touch me." I whimper.

"Yes, Princess," she says with a glimmer in her eye.

There's the Wrenn I know. That nickname makes me blush. Wrenn presses her flattened tongue across my clit and my hips rise almost a foot off the bed. I am so sensitive right now. Every time she touches me, I feel like I'm vibrating. I know how talented her tongue is and I'm waiting in anticipation. She drags her tongue through my folds, and I whimper.

"Oh, Wrenn," I mutter quietly.

She looks up at me, her eyes the only thing I can see while the rest of her face is buried deep in my pussy. God, watching a woman eat you out should be illegal. I could come from this sight alone. Her tongue is swirling, moving all over my pussy and clit. Dancing to a song I can't hear. Wrenn grips my thighs with her hands, holding me steady as she tastes me. I can feel her moaning against me.

"Yes! Right there!" I call out as I feel my orgasm crashing over me. I'm about to come, and *hard*.

Wrenn doesn't let up, letting me ride her face as I come. She only pulls away when my legs collapse on the bed and my eyes shut tight. My breathing is ragged, and I feel like I'm floating or on a boat. You know when you spend the day on a boat, but when you leave you still feel shaky? That's me. But god, does it feel good.

"I don't know what this means," she says quietly next to me. My breathing is finally steady, so I turn my head to look at her. She's staring at the ceiling, avoiding eye contact with me. Her hands are folded over her chest as she waits for me to reply.

"Wrenn Thomas, are you trying to have *the talk* with me?" I feign a gasp.

"Do not start," she grumbles.

I press my lips to her cheek, and she relaxes a bit.

"I don't know what this means any more than you do," I admit.

"But you wanted to talk about it." She looks at me, confused.

"So I could hear your thoughts and we could see what made sense for us."

"Oh." Her mouth forms a line. "I didn't realize."

"Well, that's what happens when you don't let people talk," I dig, because I can't help myself.

"I'm just not very good at the whole talking thing."

"I'm not any better. I think we both recall how I avoided this conversation last time."

"I tried to do that but I kind of fail at waking up early."

"You tried to ghost me? While we live in the same house?"

"Maybe…" She closes her eyes, then peeks one open to look at me.

"How's that going for you?"

"Well, we kept having sex. And the sex is good. So you know…"

"Is this just sex to you?"

"No. I mean at first, yeah. I was just trying to seduce you and get back at you for last year. But now…I don't know. It doesn't feel like *just* sex," Wrenn admits.

"It doesn't to me either."

"So what does that mean? Are we like, dating now?"

"Is that something you want?"

"I-I don't know. It's not like I've been in a lot of successful relationships." She sighs.

"Well, if you were in a successful relationship then we probably wouldn't be in bed together," I tease.

"Touché."

"We don't have to jump into a relationship or anything you don't want. But we admitted we have feelings for each other. We could just see where things go," I suggest.

TWENTY-ONE

Wrenn

I hesitate before saying anything to Ryleigh. I hadn't planned on coming in here tonight. I definitely didn't expect to knock on her door and end up in bed with her again. But when we came in and I kissed her, it was like something *shifted*. I don't know what, but I know I'd never figure it out on my own. So I came to her room to talk to her. Of course, then I opened my big mouth and tell her I like her. Thankfully, she said she likes me back too, or I think I would've died of embarrassment.

"Would you see other people?" I ask, thinking of the logistics of her suggestion.

"Would you?" She raises an eyebrow.

"Fuck no. I don't share well with others." I growl.

"Then I'd have no reason to." She relaxes.

"So you'd want to be in an exclusive relationship, with *me*?" I ask in disbelief.

"I'm not sure why you're surprised." She laughs.

"I mean, you and I don't have the best track record."

"I'm sorry for that. I really am—"

"You don't have to," I say, cutting her off.

"No, please let me." I nod and she continues. "I really am sorry for the way I left things with us. I was scared about Alana finding out, about what it might have meant, and I chose the easy way out. I really regret treating you that way and I'm sorry. I'll spend forever making up for it."

"I forgive you." And I do. I know that she's telling the truth here.

"So, are you going to be my girlfriend or are we going to have to fight?" she asks with a smile on her face.

"Come on, Princess, that's not how you ask someone out." I laugh.

"Well then, show me how it's done." She shakes her head.

"Ryleigh," I take her hand, sitting up in bed. "Will you be my girlfriend?" I throw in a wink for good measure, and she blushes her usual cherry red.

"Fuck, alright, that is how you ask. Yes please."

"Atta girl," I praise and press my lips to hers.

"Mmm, wait. What are we doing about your sister?"

"My sister? You really wanna talk about her right now?" I groan.

"Well, yes. Only because I've been scared shitless every time you give me a hickey that she'll figure out it was you."

I laugh. "Do you really think she'll care?"

"She's my *best* friend. You're her *sister*. Of course she'll care."

"Well, then she'll just have to get over it. I mean if we're happy then who cares?"

"Okay."

"Okay?"

"Yeah. But only if we agree to tell her together."

"Fine, but the when of it we can talk about another time."

"Deal." Ryleigh smiles and slides into my arms.

Her lips brush against mine before trailing down my neck. She takes her time to nibble on my earlobe and blow softly in my ear. I moan lightly as she runs her hands over my breasts. She unhooks my bra and tosses it to the side. Stopping to play with my piercings, tugging on them.

"God, I love your tits." Ryleigh praises.

"Mmm." I groan as she puts one in her mouth. Her tongue swirls over my nipple, then her teeth graze it gently.

Ryleigh kisses down my stomach until she gets to my hips. I watch as she unbuttons my jeans and tosses them on the floor. She smiles, looking at my pussy, I'm sure it's because of the unholy wet spot on my panties. I can't help it, she is fucking hot, and I get turned on making her come. I could spend the day eating her out if my jaw wouldn't get so tired.

"I can't wait to taste you," she whispers before cupping my pussy with her hand.

"Yes please." I moan.

She smiles, pushing my panties to the side and exposing my pussy. Ryleigh dips her head and gives me a few teasing licks. I'm patient but it's killing me. She lifts my legs, slipping my panties down my legs, and I kick them off. Ryleigh grabs a pillow, tells me to lift my hips and places it under my lower back. Then she leans between my thighs and places each leg on her shoulder. I'm flexible so it doesn't hurt, but god, when she plunges two fingers inside me, I moan.

"Holy shit." I whimper.

Ryleigh moves her fingers inside me while her tongue works magic on my clit. I close my eyes, unable to focus as she touches me. She knows exactly what I like and how rough to be. Her fingers hit my g-spot every time and she sucks hard on my clit. I'm moaning louder than I ever do, but I can't help it. I feel comfortable with her.

"Fuck," I mutter as she pulls out her fingers just to plunge them back in.

She hums against my clit. I swear I'm going to come in record time if she keeps that up. I grab my boobs, tugging on my nipples and I curse. Ryleigh's tongue is working overtime, and I can feel the heat rising in my belly.

"Oh, I'm so close!" I call out. I can feel Ryleigh smile against me, and with a flick of her tongue I'm screaming her name.

"Oh, fuck! Fuck Ryleigh! Yes!"

Ryleigh doesn't let up until I push her away and let my legs fall to the bed. She smirks at me as she licks her fingers clean. God, why is that so fucking hot? She leans over and places soft kisses on my lips, my cheeks, and my forehead. My heart is still racing but I feel calm next to her. She cuddles in my arms, and I relax against her.

"Once I catch my breath, I'm doing you again," I warn her.

"I was thinking...maybe we could try something?" She chews on her bottom lip.

"Like what?"

She reaches in her nightstand and pulls out a red butt plug with a diamond on the end.

"You want to put that in me?" I raise an eyebrow. I wasn't the biggest fan of anything going in my ass.

"No, I was hoping you'd put it in me. And fuck me with your strap on." Ryleigh turns bright red, but her confidence doesn't waver.

"Hell yes. Let me go get it." I all but jump out of the bed to go get the strap.

I'm back in record time, sliding it on while Ryleigh is holding the red butt plug and a bottle of lube. I swear she has a way of surprising me. I never would've pegged her for someone who liked ass play.

"Is this okay?" she asks.

"Oh yes. As long as nothing is going in my ass, I'm happy to be a part of this."

"Got it, no ass stuff for you." She giggles.

"Can I put it in?" I ask, looking at the toy.

"Sure, just make sure there's enough lube."

"Gotcha, I'll go slow."

I take the toy and the lube from her, watching as she kneels on the bed and puts her ass in the air. She holds her ass open to me and I groan. Why am I suddenly very into this? I climb on the bed, dip my head into her pussy, and lick her a few times. She is still *soaked*. I tease her a little with my tongue to give her a chance to relax. When she's moaning for me, I pick up the bottle of lube and drip some on her puckered hole. She groans needily, and I pour a little more before touching her and sliding a finger inside her.

"Oh!" She bucks forward and I smile. Shit, she is even more responsive.

I give her a moment to adjust, then I add more lube and pick up the toy. Sliding out my finger, I press the toy in slowly. Ryleigh moans under me and the more I push it in, the louder she gets. Once it's in, I admire how hot she looks with the shiny toy in her ass. Who knew I'd be into this?

"Can I fuck you, Princess?" I ask, running my fingers through her folds again.

"Y-yes please."

I align my hips at her waist, holding the strap on to guide me inside her. She gasps as I push my hips forward and slide inside. Gripping her back, I watch as she moans even louder for me with each movement. I don't know how it feels to have both a plug and a strap on in you, but god, Ryleigh is definitely enjoying herself. She whimpers as I thrust my hips. Each sound is like fuel to the flame. I just want to hear more.

"God, you're so fucking hot." I groan as I fuck her.

I touch her shiny toy and she whimpers. I guess it's just as sensitive.

"Wrenn! I'm, fuck. I feel so full," she cries out.

I moan and reach around to feel her breasts in my hands. I take her sensitive peaks and tug on them. Ryleigh gasps, and I smile. She is fucking close, and I'm about to send her over the edge. I twist her nipples and she screams, coming all over me.

"Oh god! Yes I'm gonna—"

Ryleigh squirts all over me. Her pussy explodes sweet juices as I continue fucking her. She moans, and I don't stop until she goes limp on the bed. I pull out gently so she can relax. She lays face down with her ass in the air and catches her breath. I slowly ease the toy out of her, and she gasps at the contact.

"Stay right here," I tell her, and I retreat to the bathroom. I clean off the toys and leave them on a clean towel to dry.

I grab some fresh sheets from the laundry room closet and bring them back to her. She's laying on the opposite side of the bed now, a huge wet spot on the other side. She blushes when she sees me.

"Sorry about the mess," she mumbles.

"Hey, don't be sorry. You can ruin the sheets anytime, Princess." I grab her face and kiss her.

"Can we sleep in your room tonight?" she asks.

"That's a good idea, I'll put these in the wash. We can remake the bed tomorrow."

I place the clean sheets on her dresser, rip off the dirty sheet, and carry it to the laundry room. When I come back, Ryleigh is in a long T-shirt and pulling her dark hair into a messy bun. Somehow, she's never looked sexier.

"Are you tired?"

"No," she says with a yawn.

"Liar." I laugh. "Let's go to bed."

I take Ryleigh's hand and lead her to my room. Cheeto is sleeping on the floor in the corner so at least we don't bother her. I grab a T-shirt and some panties. Then I slide into bed next to Ryleigh and click off the lamp. She takes me in her arms, and I yawn. I wasn't tired until my head hit the pillow and the weight of the day hit me.

"I'm glad we talked."

"Me too," I admit.

"I'm glad you're my girlfriend."

"I'm glad you're my girlfriend too." I smile.

Ryleigh eases into an easy sleep while I play with her hair. It's mindless while I twirl her hair into curls and let them go. I yawn again but I can't seem to fall asleep. It's like I'm buzzing with excitement from the night. Part of me is worried if I fall asleep right now, I will wake up tomorrow and this will all be a dream. I think I'm afraid I'll find myself alone in bed again. But then Ryleigh pulls me closer in her sleep. Her arms wrap around me, and I snuggle in closer to her. Placing a small kiss on her cheek, I finally relax enough to fall asleep.

TWENTY-TWO

Ryleigh

When I wake in the morning, it takes me a moment to remember where I am. Wrenn's arms are wrapped around my body from behind and she's spooning me. Her body is warm, the sheet over us but the blanket kicked to the floor. I smile, thinking about last night. We finally talked and got on the same page. Instead of wondering what last night means, I know exactly what it is. Cheeto climbs on the bed and licks my cheek before climbing over to Wrenn. She licks her forehead, and Wrenn wrinkles her nose.

"Good morning," she says, peeking her eyes open. I face her, and she kisses me softly on the lips.

"Good morning."

She closes her eyes and then opens them again. She yawns and then stretches her free arm.

"Did you sleep okay?"

"Yeah, your bed is comfortable."

"Good, I did too. It's much better when you're here."

Cheeto purrs, and Wrenn groans. "Okay, I have to get her some breakfast."

My stomach growls and we both laugh.

"Okay, I should get you both some food."

Wrenn and I climb out of bed and head to the kitchen. I make a stop at the bathroom to pee and meet her at the coffee maker. Cheeto is in the corner eating her breakfast. So I look in the fridge and decide to make some French toast.

"I thought I was making breakfast," Wrenn complains.

"Yeah, I want something besides eggs and cereal," I tease.

"Then I should pay attention because I have no clue how to make French toast." She laughs.

I grease the frying pan, grab a bowl for the ingredients, and start working. Meanwhile Wrenn wraps her arms around my waist and looks over my shoulder. I place the soaked bread on the pan, and she starts kissing my neck. She grabs my breast and kisses me softly. I'm having a hard time focusing on breakfast.

"It's going to burn." I groan.

"So?" Wrenn's eyes sparkle.

"How about we eat first and then we fuck until the house burns down, okay?"

"Ugh, fine," Wrenn says with a laugh.

"Can you grab my phone? I think I left it in my room."

"Sure." Wrenn disappears.

When she returns, I'm flipping the French toast. I take my phone from her and scroll through my notifications. Most of them aren't important, but a text from Alana makes me anxious. It isn't anything serious, she's just asking if I have any leftover lace from the invites. But suddenly I feel stressed about seeing her.

How am I going to tell her I'm dating her little sister? Someone we both grew up with. Is she going to freak out and never talk to me again? Will she not care like Wrenn said? It's hard to tell which way things might go. She's also so stressed about the wedding. Am I supposed to tell her now? I feel like it will be worse if we wait. But with everything going on, I don't want to be the one to send her over the edge.

"Uh, Princess? You're burning the French toast." Wrenn steps in front of me and flips the blackened piece of toast off the frying pan.

"I'm sorry, I got stuck in my head." I frown.

"It's alright. You okay?"

"Yeah, I was just thinking about Alana."

"Why?" Wrenn makes a face.

"I just was thinking about how we were going to tell her."

"Do you wanna talk about that?" Wrenn sighs. I can tell that she doesn't, but I don't wanna spend the rest of the day anxious about it.

"Yes please."

"Okay, first let's put on the next piece because I'm starving." I add a fresh piece to the frying pan. "Okay, what's going on?"

"I just don't know how she'll react. Like, will she be pissed at me? Angry with both of us? Then when do we tell her? She has a lot going on but what if we wait and she's upset that we didn't tell her right away?"

"Well, what are the pros and cons?" Wrenn walks to the counter, fills up a large pitcher of water, and starts watering the plants in the room.

"You water the plants?" I ask, confused.

"Yeah, almost every morning." She shrugs.

"I've never seen you do it, I was wondering how they stayed so green," I admit.

"Gotcha, so pros of telling Alana now?"

"Pros, she can't be upset we waited. Maybe she'll be happy for us."

"Cons?"

"I don't know. She could be upset about it and that it's so close to the wedding. I don't wanna stress her out."

"I'm afraid to tell her about it so soon, honestly," Wrenn says.

"Why?"

"It's a little too real for me." Wrenn pauses. "I'm not saying we can't tell her. It just is scary to admit to someone that we're doing this. It's like, vulnerable."

"We can wait if you think that's best."

"I think if you would feel less anxious about it then we should get it over with. Bite the bullet, rip the bandage off, etcetera."

I pause to think about it. Flipping the toast so it doesn't burn this time, I place a fresh piece in. No one is going to eat the burnt piece and we have enough bread to make more.

"I think I wanna do that. Just get it over with so it's not hanging over our heads."

"Okay, then you say when and we'll go."

I glance at my phone. "What about today?"

"Okay." Wrenn shrugs like I've asked her what she wants to eat. Like it doesn't matter. Why couldn't I be like that about this?

"But I have one request," Wrenn adds.

"Which is?"

"Once we tell my sister, you go on a date with me. A real one, in public where I can hold your hand and kiss you."

"I'd like that." I smile.

"Really?"

"Yes. It would be nice to show you off to the world."

Wrenn walks over and kisses me, a quick peck on the lips so we wouldn't forget about the food. I hand her a plate of French toast drizzled it in syrup and powdered sugar. She's moaning into her food while I grab myself a plate. Wrenn smiles at me, and I feel my stomach doing backflips. Now that I'm letting my feelings for her out of the cage I built, I can relax.

"Hey, I didn't expect to see you both today." Alana smiles as she opens the front door to her house with Will. I'm not sure when they moved in, but it is beautiful. It's a massive house as big as the homes on the estates.

"We were in the neighborhood." Wrenn shrugs. Alana gives her a hug and Wrenn grumbles, hugging her back.

"Well, come on in. But the place is a mess."

"Alana, there isn't even a mug out of place." I laugh, walking into her kitchen. The only thing that is slightly messy is the stack of papers she has on the kitchen table.

She waves me off. "Can I get you anything to drink?"

"Got any whiskey?" Wrenn jokes.

"It's not five o'clock." Alana gives her a look. "What's up?"

Maybe Wrenn and I should've rehearsed this on the car ride over. Not that we would've had more than five minutes to prepare. I look at Wrenn, who sighs and grabs my hand. Alana's eyes widen as she starts to think about it.

"Ryleigh and I are dating," Wrenn says aloud.

"I knew it!" Alana slams the counter with one hand. "I freaking knew it!"

I can't tell if her reaction is happy or mad. And what did she mean, she knew it?

"I wish I bet someone because I'd be so rich right now." She laughs.

"Why would you bet on us?" Wrenn relaxes.

"I thought there was something going on when you were sleeping in the same bed that day I came over. Especially with the hickies on Ryleigh's neck. But then you guys threw me off by saying you were seeing Shelly, and you were seeing someone new." She looks at both of us.

"I was never seeing Shelly. I just let you think I was," Wrenn clarifies.

"Same here…"

"So this has been happening, what? All summer?" Alana raises an eyebrow.

"Pretty much." Wrenn shrugs. We agreed it was better to leave out the fact that this started over a year ago.

"We just talked about being together, romantically, last night though," I clarify.

"I see," Alana muses.

"I thought we should tell you. We didn't want to keep anything from you. But I was also worried about stressing you out so close to the wedding," I admit.

"I'm glad you told me. I'm happy for you guys."

"You are?" I ask, surprised.

"Of course! I know you're going to take care of her. You're my best friend. I couldn't imagine anyone better to be with my sister." She smiles and walks over to hug me. "But if you break her heart, I'll hurt you myself," Alana whispers in my ear.

"I heard that." Wrenn laughs.

"I won't hurt her." I smile at Wrenn.

"Good." Alana nods.

"Alana? Have you seen my blue tie?" A deep voice carries from the hallway.

"Will! We have company," Alana calls back.

Will steps into the kitchen with an unbuttoned, light blue shirt and a pair of dress pants. He stops short when he sees Wrenn and I are here.

"Hello, sorry about that. I'm headed to a work function, and I cannot find my tie. How are you both doing?" Will smiles at both of us. He's handsome, I'll give Alana that. He's at least six four, has an athletic build and a clean-cut face with sparkling blue eyes.

"It's in the laundry room, I'll grab it." Alana smiles before disappearing.

"Good." Wrenn smiles.

"Wrenn, we haven't seen you at family dinners in a bit," Will adds.

"When my family stops going to family dinners, I'll be sure to join," Wrenn jokes. Will laughs just as Alana is back in the room.

"Here." Alana stands in front of Will, loosening his collar and putting on his tie.

As she ties it for him, it's hard not to notice the way Will looks at her. He smiles, but his eyes are somehow smiling too. He looks at her like something out of a movie. Maybe I have nothing to worry about with them after all. I mean, weddings are stressful. But then I glance at Alana, and while she does his tie, I don't think she even notices Will. Her face is flat, like she could be helping anyone. Not someone she's about to marry in a few weeks.

"Did you stop by for some wedding duties or is this a fun visit?" Will ponders.

"Wrenn and Ryleigh actually stopped by to tell me they're dating," Alana explains.

"How awesome! I think you called that one, didn't you babe? I could've sworn you said something was up."

"I knew I did!" Alana laughs.

"Well, I have to get going, but it was great seeing you both." Will kisses Alana quickly on the lips before heading back into the bedroom.

"Well, since you're here, can you help with some wedding stuff?" Alana asks hopefully.

Wrenn groans and I silently elbow her in the ribs. If Alana is asking for help, we should help. Besides, what can she possibly have us do that is worse than stuffing envelopes? Thankfully, she only needs the silverware for the wedding reception to be folded in the napkins she bought. She says something about it being the perfect color for the wedding. She goes on a tangent about how she thought she rented some from the caterer, but they have no record of that so this is a last minute task. I kind of tune her out while we work, mainly because Wrenn looks so cute when she is concentrating. She is in focus mode, trying to fold the napkins correctly and only gets it after the third time I show her.

TWENTY-THREE

Wrenn

GIA:

WRENN are you there??

RONNIE:

I haven't heard from her in a bit.

ALYSSA:

Me either.

GIA:

IS SHE GOOD?!

RONNIE:

Is she mad?

ALYSSA:

Why would she be mad?

GIA:

Last time we saw her we called her out for liking the roommate she 'hates.'

ALYSSA:

…but that's true.

Gia and Ronnie emphasized Alyssa's message

Wrenn is typing...

GIA:

SHE'S ALIVE!

ME:

I'm not mad. Just been busy and I keep forgetting my phone at home.

RONNIE:

How can that be?

ALYSSA:

My phone is glued to my hand.

WRENN:

Well, maybe you guys were right...

Gia and Alyssa questioned Wrenn's message

WRENN:

I might be dating said roommate...

GIA:

😱😱😱

RONNIE:

I KNEW IT!!!

ME:

Yeah, yeah. We keep hearing that...

ALYSSA:

Are you happy?

ME:

Yeah, happier than I've been in a long time. I'm myself with her.

* Gia, Ronnie & Alyssa Loved Wrenn's message*

GIA:

When do we get to meet her??

ME:

Soon! But tonight is our first official date, gotta go!

I have been pretty wrapped in Ryleigh lately. I need to make time this week to see my friends. I don't want to be one of those girls who got a girlfriend and forgot about her friends.

"Are you ready to go?" Ryleigh walks in the living room where I'm sitting on the couch, waiting.

"Yes." My eyes rake over her body. She's wearing a white crop top and a long floral print skirt that has a slit up the thigh. When she turns to put her sneakers on, I check out her perfectly round ass.

"You look at me like that and we'll never make it out of here," she warns me.

"You're right." I look at her and kiss her lips.

"Can I drive?"

"Only if you promise not to hit my car on the way out of the driveway," I tease.

"Come on, are we really still talking about that?" She groans.

"Hey, I like my little dent. It reminds me of the first time I saw you this summer."

"Yeah, and you looked like you wanted to kill me."

"That's not how I remember it." I wink as I slide in the passenger side of her car.

"I'm giving you the aux as long as you play at least one Jo-Bros song on the way." She hands me the cord and I laugh.

"Deal." I smile.

I won't admit it to her, but they are kind of growing on me. I mean, after hearing them every time we get in the car, you either go crazy or love them.

"You do need to tell me where we're going." She hands me her phone with the map app open.

I type in the address of the mini golf place that is in the town over. They have the best food, and the course is used at night for adults.

"Mini golf?! That's so fun!" She squeals, recognizing the address.

"Let's go, we have a reservation for eight p.m."

Ryleigh starts driving and I look for a playlist to put on. Eventually I find one that has Jonas Brothers and other hit songs from the last decade. I'm humming along, watching Ryleigh drive. I don't even notice when we get to the place.

"You coming? Or too afraid I'll kick your ass?" She smirks.

"No chance." I laugh.

Running out of the car, I race to the front booth and scan my phone. A man hands us each a golf club and a ball. I let Ryleigh go first, but the whole time she's getting ready to go, I heckle her. Yelling out to miss, getting close to her and then backing up. Hoping that she'll miss her shot.

"HEY! You're not playing fair!" she yells.

"Who said I played fair, Princess?"

Ryleigh's eyes darken with desire, and I laugh. She bends her hips, hits the pink ball and gets a hole in one. Fuck. I guess I didn't do such a good job of distracting her.

"Ha!" she says proudly.

I step up to the putt and focus on the zone. I'm about to hit the ball when she sneezes. I hit the ball, and it goes right past the hole and into the water.

"You did that on purpose!"

"I had to sneeze!" She puts her hands up in defense.

"Uh huh." I give her a fake glare and she blows me a kiss.

I do the walk of shame to the office and ask for another ball. Ryleigh waits for me at the second hole and I watch as she lines up perfectly to get another hole in one. What the fuck? I want to be happy for her, but dammit, I'm competitive as hell. I didn't think she'd give me a run for my money. When I get the shot on the tenth swing, I'm starting to lose faith in myself. By the time we're on the ninth hole and Ryleigh has a perfect score, I think I'm being punk'd.

"Is this for a Tik Tok? Am I being live streamed right now?!" I ask Ryleigh.

"No! I swear." She giggles.

"How the hell are you so good?" I groan.

"My parents used to take me here on the weekends as a kid. I've sort of mastered this course as time went on."

"Why didn't you say anything?"

"I wanted to win." She shrugs.

"God, if you weren't my girlfriend you'd so be dead right now." I glare. Ryleigh leans in to kiss me and I relax. God, I hate when she does that.

"What if I give you some pointers?"

"I do not need pointers." I scoff.

"If you let me help you, I'll put my arms around you and kiss your neck," she whispers in my ear.

"Oh." I smile. "Okay, teach me everything you know."

"Okay, so you want to bend a little more," Ryleigh says, looking at my stance.

I move a little and then she's behind me, her arms around me to touch the golf club. I feel her warm body against mine, and she moves my hair out of the way so she can see me better. We raise our arms together, and this time I actually get a hole in one. Turning around, I give her a kiss on the lips.

"Come on." She leads me to the next hole and with her help, I do better. I don't get any more holes in one, but at least I'm not losing anymore balls in the water.

On the last hole, Ryleigh gets it on two shots. I lose my ball somewhere in the grass, so I give up and decide it's time for us to eat. We order way too much food. My eyes are bigger than my stomach when I'm hungry. There's waffle fries, regular fries, hamburgers, and hotdogs.

"I don't think we can eat all of this," Ryleigh says, shoving a fry in her mouth.

"Probably not. But we can take any of it home."

"We can have cold fries in the middle of the night after sex."

"Sex? On the first date?" I feign a gasp, and Ryleigh tosses a fry at me.

"Oh, shush you."

"Make me." I wiggle my eyebrows, and she blushes.

"Don't you start. We're in *public!*" she whisper-yells at me.

I shrug and take a bite of the hotdog. I'm just messing with her, but it is honestly way too easy to rile her up. We end up taking most of the fries home, and Ryleigh puts them in the fridge the second we get there. She disappears into the bedroom, so I feed Cheeto her dinner and wait for her to come out. When she finally reappears, my jaw drops to the floor. Ryleigh is standing before me in nothing but the thinnest piece of lace on her pussy and the handcuffs hanging off her finger.

"I thought we could go for a midnight swim."

"Huh?" I didn't hear a word she said. I was too busy staring at her gorgeous body.

"Come on." She giggles and takes my hand.

She leads me outside, and I stop to get undressed. Completely naked, I follow her into the pool. She tosses the handcuffs on the edge of the pool and dives in. She swims up to the edge of the pool, grabs the handcuffs and looks at me. I dive in and swim to where she is.

"I wanna cuff you and fuck you under the water."

"Yes, please." I groan. Who the hell would say no to something like that?

She takes my hands, wraps them behind me, and cuffs my wrists together. Smiling, she leans in to kiss me. Her tongue swipes across my lips, then she nibbles on my bottom lip. She slides her tongue in my mouth, and I lose control. Maybe I don't fight for it, because for once, I don't care if Ryleigh has it. God, I *want* her to have it. Being in the water adds another level of trust to this. Sure, I can stand over here but it's not like I could get out without her.

"You're so beautiful," she whispers, holding my face.

I look away and she pulls my face back to hers. I look in her dark eyes, and she makes me feel things. Things I don't think I've ever felt before. Her wet hair glistens in the moonlight, the stars shining around her. *She* is the beautiful one.

Ryleigh pushes me back against the wall of the pool. Her body against mine. Her perky breasts press against my pierced nipples. I don't move, afraid if I do, she'll stop touching me, and that's the last thing I want right now. She grabs my breast in her hand, flicks the metal bar, and I whimper. Fuck, that felt good. Ryleigh's hand dips under the water, and she cups my pussy. Her fingers run through my folds, and I moan.

"Oh, yes." She smiles.

I assume she's going to tease me, but instead she drags her fingers through my pussy and then slides them in. It's at least three at once, so I buck forward and groan.

"You like that?"

"God, yes!" I moan.

Ryleigh looks pleased with herself, so she starts to move her fingers. Curling them inside me, she begins to move them in and out. I have no idea what she is doing, but it feels great. Her lips move to my neck, biting gently and nibbling on the nape of my neck. I toss my head back against the wall and close my eyes. The warm water pushes against me as Ryleigh moves her hand faster and faster inside me.

"I want you to come for me," she commands.

"Yes, Princess."

Ryleigh moves her hand faster, and I rock my hips against her. She bites my neck, and I cry out her name. "Oh, Ryleigh!"

She keeps kissing my neck, kissing my lips, and with a flick of her thumb across my clit, I'm coming. I lose control of my body, and Ryleigh uses her spare hand to keep me from drowning. All I feel is pure bliss as my legs go limp under me. My eyes shut tight, and I see actual stars. When I open them again, I'm a little dizzy. Ryleigh works to uncuff me and kisses my lips softly.

"Are you okay?" she asks.

"I'm a little dizzy," I admit. Her eyes widen.

"Come on." She rushes to help me out of the pool, bringing me to the chairs on the side and sitting me down. "Wait right here."

I nod, which is a bad idea because my head is spinning. I'm afraid I'm going to pass out when Ryleigh returns with a bottle of water and the leftover fries.

"I figured you needed something salty and something to hydrate you," she explains.

"You must've known these fries would come in handy," I tease as I pop one in my mouth. I chug half the bottle of water, and I start to feel normal again.

TWENTY-FOUR

Ryleigh

It's the day of Alana's bachelorette party, so I spent the morning putting the final touches on the gift bags. Everything is ready for the night, so I sneak away to the art room to work on a painting. I've been painting every morning when Wrenn gets out of bed to go for her daily swim. We thought it was important that we kept our routines so we don't lose ourselves in the relationship. Of course, we are no longer using my bedroom. I spend every night with Wrenn, usually naked and between her legs. But the mornings are our alone time. Since I have used mine differently this morning, I sneak in here now while Wrenn is getting ready. I still have an hour until I have to get ready, and I am itching to draw something. I use my iPad since I already showered and setting up paint would take way too long.

I curl up on the couch, a blanket on my lap and my cardigan wrapped around me. I begin to relax with each line. I'm drawing Wrenn for no one but myself. I've been wanting to draw her, like really draw her, for a bit now. But she's usually around, and I don't want her to see it. So I draw her from memory because she's the only thing on my mind. I get all the details of her face, her long purple hair, the small birthmark on her cheek. I'm so busy drawing that I almost don't see Wrenn come in.

"What do you think? This one or that one?" Wrenn holds up two different black dresses while standing in her underwear.

"The middle," I tease, choosing her naked.

"I'm serious. I can't decide." She groans.

I look at both dresses. Either way she is going to look hot as fuck, but the one on the left shows more boob so I pick that one. Wrenn disappears and I look at the clock. Shit, it's time for me to get ready now. I leave my iPad behind and get dressed. Hair and makeup are done so it's just a matter of putting on my black dress.

Alana had specified that she would be wearing a white mini dress, and we should all be wearing black. It's simple enough and everyone looks good in black so no one complains. I kick on my heels when Wrenn stands in the doorway, now fully dressed.

"Shit, are you not wearing a bra?" I groan, looking at her chest.

"It didn't look right with one." She shrugs.

"Lucky me."

Leaning in, I kiss her slowly. Before we get too carried away and end up ditching the party, I pull back. Wrenn groans but goes to grab her purse. Norah is driving us over since she offered to be one of the designated drivers of the night. Of course, everyone just thought she was being nice when in reality, she needs a good cover for not drinking.

"They're here!" Wrenn calls, and we head outside.

Norah and Gemma are in the front seats, so Wrenn and I pile in the back.

"Seatbelts everyone," Norah reminds us.

"Yes mom," I tease. Her eyes widen thinking I've given up her secret but relax when she realizes I'm just joking.

Gemma and I had been to Teddy's earlier to bring everything over. Wrenn secured the place for the night and all of the women who are under forty and friends with Alana were invited. Which means it is going to be crazy packed.

When we get there, it's easy to spot Alana, she's the only one dressed in white. The rest of the girls are in black, while any other guests are in a mix of colors. Everyone is drinking and there are waiters going around the room offering shots. The place looks amazing considering how it normally looks.

"Would ya look who it is." Kim notices me holding hands with Wrenn.

"Oh shush." I pull her in for a hug. She acts like she's surprised when in reality, she was the first person I called the minute I was alone.

"I'm happy to see things worked out." She smiles.

"Okay they gave me tequila and I hate tequila; someone needs to drink this." Heather walks over with her bright pink hair and a camera around her neck.

"Give me!" I take the glass from her and wince as it goes down.

"Shit, no chaser?" Wrenn looks impressed.

"Now hug me! I missed you!" Heather is probably drunk off her ass but she's smiling and having a good time.

"I'm Sage by the way, Heather's girlfriend." The dark-haired butch steps forward and offers us a hand. I recognized her from Heather's Instagram, but I didn't know she was coming tonight.

"It's nice to meet you, I'm Ryleigh and this is my girlfriend Wrenn."

"Wrenn, the sister of the bride, right?" Sage asks, trying to piece it together.

"Yup." Wrenn nods.

"How much has she had?" I glance at Heather, whispering to Sage.

"Enough. She just had some water so she's pacing herself. I'm only having a seltzer, so I have an eye on her," Sage reassures me. She looks over at Heather and smiles when their eyes meet.

"I brought my camera! Everyone get together!" Heather instructs. She puts her camera up to her face but frowns. The lens cap is still on, but I don't think she realizes.

"Why is it coming out black?" she grumbles. Sage steps forward, pops off the cap, and slips it in her pocket.

"God, isn't my girlfriend so smart?" Heather gushes and takes the picture.

"I need a drink and to say hi to the bride." Wrenn and I excuse ourselves to head to the bar.

Once we each have a drink in our hands, I look around for Alana. She's in the corner with Gemma playing shot roulette, a game where you don't know what shot you get until you're drinking it. People are gathered around her, watching and cheering her on as she downs four shots in a row without making a face.

Gemma hands her a basket of fries and Norah gives her a glass of water. At least someone is taking care of her tonight.

"Oh god, drunk Alana is the worst." Wrenn groans.

"Why?" I laugh. I love when my friends get drunk.

"She just tells me she loves me over and over and is way too clingy." Wrenn rolls her eyes.

"We *have* to say hello, it's her night," I remind her. Wrenn grumbles but follows me over.

"Oh my gosh! Hi guys! Look Gemma, it's my sister and my bestie! They're dating, isn't that SO cute?" Alana hangs over us and I laugh. While Wrenn shoots me an *I told you so* look.

"How's everything?" I ask.

"So fun! Oh my gosh, you should totally do some shots with me!" Alana picks one up and puts it in my hand before I can reply.

I shrug, down the shot, and wince at the taste of the cinnamon whiskey. God, that tastes like college and bad memories. Alana hands me another one and this time we do it together. It's another shot of tequila, so I don't choke on this one.

"Did you meet Heather's new girlfriend? She's kind of hot," Alana whisper-yells in my ear.

"I did meet her." I'm careful not to agree too quickly. Sure, Sage is hot, but she has nothing on Wrenn.

"I'll be right back." Wrenn disappears into the crowd, so I turn to talk to Gemma, Alana, and Norah.

"It's STRIPPER TIME," someone yells and the crowd cheers.

Then, in the middle of the room, a circle clears to make way for Chris Matthews. He was Prom King in high school and now was the town's stripper for all events. He's dressed in a suit and smiles when he spots Alana.

"I thought I said no strippers!" She gasps. But she's giggling underneath her distaste.

Chris leads Alana down the middle of the room, sits her on the chair that someone put there, and puts down his stuff.

"I heard someone was getting married!" he yells, and the room cheers.

Those shots went right to my head because I'm drunk already. Wrenn comes back to my side, wrapping an arm around my waist while she sips on a new drink. I sip on the one I had before all the shots and drown out the taste of the bad ones.

Chris starts giving Alana a lap dance and cheering all around the room begins. He takes off his shirt, and might I say, those are some impressive abs. Alana is blushing harder than I've ever seen before, trying to cover her eyes while also peeking. He tosses his pants off and throws his tie at her. She grabs it and puts it on over her head. I hope Heather or someone was grabbing photo evidence of this.

When he's finally done with the show, he joins us for the party. Everyone is dancing and drinking the night away. Wrenn grinds on me as the music heats up, and I can feel my heart pulsing in my chest. The floor was vibrating from all the dancing, and I'm feral for my girl. She kisses me hard and fast. Her lips taste like vodka, and I get drunk off the taste. I can't stop kissing her.

"Come with me." She grabs me by the hand and leads me to some back room I've never been in before.

I don't get a second to look around because she's back to kissing me. With her body against mine, I reach for her soft tits. She slides a thigh in between my legs, and I grind against it. My clit hits it hard, trying to get off on the friction she's providing. Wrenn starts kissing and biting my neck. She's probably leaving marks, but I don't care. It feels too fucking good to care. I moan loudly, but no one can hear me. The music is too loud and so are the people.

"God, you're so beautiful," she murmurs against my skin.

"I need you babe," I moan out.

"I need you too, Princess."

Wrenn kisses me, biting down on my bottom lip and dragging it toward her. I moan in her mouth, grind against her, and fall into a drunken bliss. To think, we started this because of a drunken hookup over a year ago. Now here I am, ready to give her everything. I'm falling in love with Wrenn, there is no doubt about it. She makes me feel calm in all the ways I never have before. She pushes me to be competitive and to win as much as possible. She sees who I am and never strays. As much as I want to blurt it out right now, I know it isn't the time. I want the first time I tell her I love her to be special. I want us both to remember it. And I want to be absolutely sure, not just filled with lust and alcohol. So I stay quiet and enjoy how amazing it feels to be with Wrenn in this moment.

"I hate how much you turn me on," she grumbles.

"No, you don't. You love it."

"You're right. I do."

Wrenn keeps kissing me, our bodies melting into each other. We are too drunk to go all the way right now, but god, just feeling her lips on mine? I could do this forever.

Eventually, we pull ourselves apart long enough to go back to the party, not that anyone noticed we were gone. We have plenty of time to hook up. For now, I want to show off my girlfriend to everyone and anyone who'll listen. She is mine and I'm hers. Thank god, she is such a stubborn ass and seduced me this summer. I can't imagine what my life might be like if she hadn't.

Epilogue I

WRENN

1 year later...

"**W**hat the hell is in these boxes?" I complain as I pick up another of Ryleigh's boxes.

"I don't know, I think that's just my art supplies." Ryleigh smiles.

"I guess I should be grateful you're not a big reader or these boxes would be even heavier." I tease.

"And we downsized a lot of our stuff before we started traveling too." She reminds me.

Ryleigh and I spent most of the last year traveling all over the world together. We visited all the places I've never been to and some of the places Ryleigh already loved. After Alana's not wedding, we packed up all our stuff into a storage center and went adventuring together. Ryleigh was making crazy money now that she was taking on custom work from clients and was able to work wherever she wanted as it was mostly digital. I had started online journalism classes with her encouragement.

"Have you guys seen Alana since you got back?" Heather asks popping out from behind the moving truck.

"No, but we're having dinner together tomorrow night. She

said she has stuff she wants to talk about." I shrug. When my sister pulled a runaway bride act a year ago on her fiancé, she surprised everyone. So whatever she wanted to talk about couldn't be crazier than that.

"When do we get to see your new place?" Ryleigh asks Heather and Sage. They just moved in together a few months ago when we were away.

"Anytime, just be sure to knock first. Maeve made that mistake last week." Sage adds with a wink.

"You two aren't even married yet, how can you be so bad?" Ryleigh laughs.

The couple shrugs and carries the last of the boxes into the truck. I climb in the drivers seat with Ryleigh next to me. They were taking the breakable smaller items in the car to our new place. So I take Ryleigh's hand as we drive to our new place.

The house wasn't huge, but it was perfect for us. I had spent most of my life in big houses and too many rooms. So when we found this place, I knew it was what we needed. A two bedroom house with a pool in the backyard. The second bedroom had beautiful natural lighting and would be Ryleigh's art studio. It didn't overlook the pool like at the estate, but it would do.

"Are you ready?" I smile at Ryleigh and she nods.

"I can't wait to start decorating the place." She says with hearts in her eyes.

I was excited to see her make our place, a *home*.

We pull up and I grab a lighter box, heading inside to put Cheeto in her crate. She hated going in it but I didn't want to risk her escaping while we were moving in. I give her some of her favorite treats and a new toy and she relaxes enough for me to grab the rest of our stuff.

"Cheeto's all safe in our bedroom." I smile. *Our* bedroom. I loved the way that sounded. After a year of hotel rooms and hostels being our room, it was nice to actually call something totally ours.

We had a moving company bring all our furniture, most of it

new, to the house last weekend. That way we could move in our boxes with ease. Most of it was put together by now and just needed our things to finish it.

"Let's just bring all the boxes in and then we can figure out unpacking later on?" Ryleigh suggests.

"Sounds good to me." I nod.

The four of us take the next several hours to unpack the truck and the cars. Suddenly the house feels smaller than I thought it was. Everywhere you looked was a stack of boxes and it was hard to move around. But we had gotten everything inside before it was dark and I had to return the moving truck tonight. I had left my car at the place where we rented the U-Haul so I could drive back easily.

"Do you want me to come with you?" Ryleigh asks.

"Nah, why don't you just relax? I'll bring back some pizza from the place next door and be back within the hour?" I look at Heather and Sage who smile.

"Sounds good babe." She kisses me on the lips and I snag the keys off the new key hook. One of the first things we actually put up in the place.

I drive into town, noticing how similar everything was. Even though Ryleigh and I had been gone for so long, some things never change. I didn't really want to move back to Lovers, but I knew Ryleigh did. We decided we needed to settle with some roots but that didn't mean we were done traveling. Getting a smaller place meant we had more money for traveling and we were already planning to go to Canada later this month.

I pick up the pizza after dropping off the U-Haul and drive home with two delicious smelling pies. I let myself in and Heather, Sage and Ryleigh are all sitting in the kitchen laughing about something.

"Food's here!" I shout and place the pizzas on the empty counter.

"Thank goodness, I'm starved." Heather smiles.

Everyone digs into the pizza and I head to the bedroom to let

Cheeto out. She already had dinner but now that we were done moving stuff inside, she could come out of her crate. She brushes up against my leg and purrs. She couldn't come with us on our travels, so I hadn't seen much of her the last year. Heather had taken her in for me and took care of her while we were gone. I'm glad Cheeto wasn't too upset with me now that I was back.

"Wrenn! You're missing the pizza!" Ryleigh calls.

I find her in the kitchen shoving half a slice of pizza in her mouth. I laugh at the sight of her. She was dripping pizza oil down her shirt, her hair was in a messy bun and she had permanent marker on the side of her nose. But even like this, I was enamored by her. Ryleigh was beautiful no matter what or when. Spending the better half of a year together showed me that I loved every side of her.

"Come here." I kiss her cheek and she rubs the pizza grease on my face with her nose.

"Whoops." She laughs and grabs a napkin.

"You're such a mess." I muse.

"But you love it." She smirks.

"That I do." I grab myself a slice of pizza and then wipe my face clean.

"We're going to miss having Cheeto around, we might have to get a cat ourselves." Sage says as Cheeto rubs against her leg.

"I was thinking the same thing." Heather smiles.

"I take it she didn't give you guys any trouble then?" I ask.

"Nope, if anything we didn't want to give her back. I suggested we lie and say she got lost but Heather said that wasn't fair." Sage teases.

"Uh yeah, I needed my baby back home." I'd had Cheeto for too many years now to try and part with her.

"Did you make that?" Heather asks Ryleigh, pointing to the framed painting on the wall.

"Yeah." Ryleigh says shyly with a blush. It was the painting she did of me, the first one I had caught her making last year. It was one of my favorites and I had insisted it be one of the first things we hang in our place.

"It's beautiful, you really captured her essence." Sage muses.

"I really love it." Heather adds.

"Thanks, it's easy when I have such a beautiful muse." Ryleigh smiles at me and I swear I can see the hearts in her eyes.

Epilogue II

RYLEIGH

Heather and Sage head home for the night after Wrenn and I thank them again. We had a lot more stuff than I thought we did. I'm unpacking a box while Wrenn is in the kitchen pouring us each a glass of wine. I find the box of all my records and start lining them up on one of the bookshelves in the living room. My record player is already on a table so I find the album I'm looking for and put it on. Wrenn walks in the room a minute later and puts the wine on the coffee table.

"You have to dance with me." She laughs, holding out her hand.

I take it, slipping into her arms with a smile. The Jonas Brothers 'When You Look Me in the Eyes' plays quietly behind us. I lay my head on her shoulders and we sway around our living room. Well, as much as we can with all the boxes nearby. Wrenn sways her hips and I look at her. God, she was so fucking beautiful. Gone, was the purple hair dye she used to have. Opting for her natural dark hair while we were traveling. It was much easier to maintain when we didn't know where we'd be the next week. She'd gotten her eyebrow pierced last month while we were in London. Something that suited her and made her look even more badass.

I lean in to kiss her softly. Wrenn's lips capture mine and my tongue slips in her mouth. She groans as I grab her ass in my hands and pull her body against mine. It had only been a few hours since we'd kissed but I was craving it. Craving *her*. After spending the last year together, it was weird when we weren't touching or kissing. Sure, we saw the sights. But we also made love all over the world and kissed in anyplace we could.

The song ends and we both pull apart. I grab the glass of wine and take a small sip. Mmm, it tasted just like the wine we had in Italy. I take another sip before putting the glass down. Wrenn sits on the couch, sipping her glass and watching me as I go back to unpacking records.

I finish the box I'm working on, break it down and toss it in the pile in the corner of the kitchen. I rip the tape off the next box and Wrenn jumps up from the couch yelling.

"No!"

"What?"

"You can't open that one." She says.

"What? You're kidding right?" I laugh.

"No, seriously you can't open that one." She insists.

"Uh, why?" I raise an eyebrow at her.

"You just can't." Now she's standing next to me, trying to block me from opening the box.

"Wrenn, what are you doing? Who cares if I open this box? We live together now."

"I know, but this is *my* box and I need to be the one to open it."

"That makes no sense." I cross my arms over my chest.

"Just let me open this one."

"Fine." I pause. "Then go ahead, open it."

She looks down at the box, then back at me. "Well, I don't need to open it right now."

"Jesus, Wrenn." I shove her out of the way and open the box. All while she's trying to stop me.

"I don't see what the big deal is? It's a box of your winter sweaters and…" I stop talking when I spot a small black box. Like the kind of black box you see when you're about to get proposed to.

"You saw it didn't you?" Wrenn groans when I close the lid of the box.

"Nope! I saw nothing!" I lie.

"You're such an ass sometimes." Wrenn rolls her eyes.

"I didn't know!"

"That's why I said don't open it! Sometimes you're so infuriating."

"I know."

Wrenn reaches in the box, pulls out the little black box and I gasp as she drops down to one knee. This was really happening.

"Ryleigh Hale, you both make me the happiest person on the planet and the angriest. You push all my buttons and seem to have a knack for driving me insane. But I have loved every second of it. If the last year was any indication of what the future is to bring then I cannot wait. I love you even when I don't like you. I want to spend the rest of my days being annoyed by you. Will you marry me?" She pops open the box and I squeal as I see the ring.

A beautiful oval cut diamond, almost identical to the one I fell in love with in Spain.

"Yes!" Tears start pouring down my face as she places the ring on my finger.

Wrenn stands up and pulls me in close for a kiss. Her hands wiping my wet cheeks dry.

"I love you." I mutter against her lips.

"I love you too." She kisses me again.

"Did we put sheets on the bed yet?" I murmur as our kiss deepens.

"No." Wrenn groans.

"Then how about we go christen the shower in our bedroom?"

"God, yes please."

"Race ya!" I run ahead and start stripping my clothes as I run to the bathroom.

Wrenn pushes me into the bed and I laugh as I throw my shorts to the side. We were too competitive for our own good. But If this was how the next fifty years would be, I wouldn't want to argue with anyone else.

"Beat ya!" Wrenn's standing in the shower naked in all her glory with a big smile on her face.

I think fast and turn on the shower head, blasting her with freezing cold water.

"You ass!" She squeals and tries to shut off the water but she can't without being completely immersed in it.

"I'm a sore loser, what can I say?" I laugh.

I fix the water temperature before climbing in. Wrenn pushes me against the freezing cold wall and I yelp.

"Now it's time for me to get payback for that." Wrenn says with dark eyes.

"Oh yeah? How's that?" I push her. Knowing it will only fuel the fire.

"I can think of a few ways." One of Wrenn's hands is next to my face holding onto the wall. The other, drops between my legs and she runs a fingertip through my folds.

"Fuck." Embarrassingly, I was more turned on than I should be. But Wrenn had that effect on me.

The water sprays warm droplets on our arms, my back is still freezing from the cool tile wall. But Wrenn's hand is moving circles around my clit and I can't focus on much else. Her tongue is in my ear, her warm breath teasing me as she tugs on my earlobe. Fuck. Why the hell was that so sexy?

"God, I love how wet you are for me." She whimpers in my ear.

Her breasts brush across my hardened nipples and I gasp. Her hand dips inside me and I feel her fingers curling. My legs give out and she has to steady me with her free hand.

"Now that was just too easy." She smirks and I groan. I hated letting her win, but when it came to her touching me, was I really losing?

I lean in to kiss her and our lips collide. My tongue slides inside her mouth, and we both groan. Her body presses tighter against mine and the bathroom starts to steam up from all the hot water we're using. It's like a sauna in here but that only makes me want her more.

"I think you need to earn your orgasm, since you were such a sore loser." She says against my lips.

"How?"

Wrenn pulls her hand out of me abruptly and backs away from me. "Make me cum first."

I waste no time, getting on my knees. Wrenn pushes my head against her wet pussy and I moan against her. She tastes as sweet as always, I suck on her clit and she begins to ride my face. Reaching up, I flick her piercings with my fingers.

"Fuck, Princess." Wrenn moans and I smile against her.

Sucking just a bit harder, I also slide two fingers inside her and it isn't long before she's coming and moaning my name. Nothing sounds sweeter but when I look up and see my new engagement ring on her breasts, I groan. I was making my fiancé cum loud and proud. Wrenn wasn't just my girlfriend anymore. She wanted to spend the rest of her life with me. Thank God I got my head out of my ass last year. I couldn't imagine spending my life with anyone else. Or being between anyone else's thighs.

BONUS EPILOGUE

RYLEIGH

"I'm pretty sure your sister is going to kill us if we're late on her wedding day." I point out as Wrenn moves her body down mine and settles between my thighs.

"I guess that means you need to cum quick, Princess." She smirks.

"No pressure." I laugh but it's cut off with a moan because Wrenn sticks her tongue on my clit and I forget how to breathe.

"Fuck," I groan and Wrenn slides her tongue down my slit, across my center and back around my clit.

"Mmm," She hums against me and I grip the sheets.

Wrenn had a habit of teasing me before she made me cum but since we didn't have time for that today, she was going all in. The last thing we needed was to be the reason Alana was stressed on her wedding day. She had enough going on and we could do our bridesmaids duty of being on time and ready for hair and makeup.

Wrenn slides two fingers inside me and I buck under her touch. She adds a third which she slips in my ass and I bite down on my lip so hard I'm surprised I don't draw blood. I loved it when she played with my ass. Moving her fingers in and out of me, I moan. Her tongue drags across my clit only so she can suck on it. That's all it takes and I'm moaning Wrenn's name for her.

"Fuck! Yes! Wrenn, right there!" I call out and she doesn't let up until I'm pushing her face away.

"God, I love it when you cum." She smirks. Wrenn climbs into bed next to me and pulls me into her naked arms.

"Mmm." I mumble against her skin. I could easily fall asleep right now.

"I know you're spent, but you're the one who said we have to go babe." She plays with my hair and I sigh. My eyes flutter closed and I yawn.

"Five more minutes?" I groan.

"Okay." She says and I close my eyes against her chest. I'm sleeping almost instantly.

RING!

RING!

RING!

My phone on the nightstand is going off and I groan. How long had I been out? I look over at Wrenn and see her fast asleep next to me. Fuck, what time was it? I grab my phone and can't see the time since Heather is calling me.

"Heather?"

"Ry! Thank goodness, Alana is sort of freaking out that you guys aren't here yet. Are you on your way or something?" Heather rushes.

"Uh, yes." I lie.

"Please tell me you'll be here soon. She's panicking." Heather says quietly.

I glance at the clock on the wall. "We'll be there in fifteen minutes. Stall her."

"Okay." Heather sighs a breath of relief and hangs up.

"Wrenn!" I toss a pillow at her head as I jump out of bed.

"What?" She says lazily.

"We overslept! I thought you were staying awake! I asked for five more minutes and now we're almost an hour late!" I yell. I knew we shouldn't have had sex this morning. We didn't have time for it and now Alana was going to kill us.

"Oh shit." Wrenn jumps out of bed and grabs her phone. No doubt, with a ton of missed calls from Alana.

I need to shower so I race to the bathroom and Wrenn is close behind me grabbing the towels. We take the quickest shower known to man. Thankfully we washed our hair after a bath last night so we weren't exactly gross. I'm dressed in random clothes and throwing Wrenn her's on the bed while we take turns brushing our teeth. We're out the door in ten minutes, giving us five minutes to get there. Thankfully it was just down the road from us.

"Hopefully Alana won't be too upset." Wrenn says from the passenger seat. I shoot her a death glare. "What?"

"You're joking right? It's your sister's wedding day. Of course she's going to be upset two of her bridesmaids are almost an hour late! I told you we didn't have time for sex."

"You didn't complain when you were coming." She scoffs.

"You can't be serious right now." I growl.

"I love it when you get angry with me."

"Oh no, don't try to turn me on to distract me right now." I grumble.

"Babe, come on. I'll take the blame with Alana okay? It won't be a big deal." She reaches for my hand and I sigh.

"Fine." I was still mad, but there was nothing I could do about it now.

"Finally! Where were you two!?" Alana scowls when we arrive at the bridal suite.

"It's my fault, I was supposed to set the alarm and forgot." Wrenn steps in front of me to take the brunt of it from her sister.

"Ugh, fine. Well, you're here now." She sighs.

"We're doing makeup, then hair and then getting dressed." Alana instructs and I nod. She was in a full face of makeup but her hair was in a messy bun on her head.

"Okay." We both nod and slide into the chairs in front of the mirrors.

Heather and Norah are already done and in their dresses, while Gemma and Kim are getting their hair done. Heather disappears for a bit while Norah comes to sit next to me while I get my makeup done. I can't really talk but it's nice knowing she's there. She's sipping orange juice out of a champagne glass.

"Do you want a mimosa?" She asks when I'm done with my makeup.

"I'd love one." I smile.

"Wrenn? You want one?"

"Yes please, if you don't mind." Wrenn smiles. I'm sure that gesture isn't lost on her.

Norah nods and walks to the other side of the room to grab our drinks. Wrenn's looking at me in the mirror and although I still want to be mad about making us late, it's hard when she's looking at me like that. She's smiling and has one eyebrow raised, as if to ask if I'm still angry. I smile back and she winks. God, I was falling for her more than I had anticipated.

"Here you are." Norah hands us two glasses.

"Shit, you make 'em strong." Wrenn gasps after taking a sip.

"You're both drinking for me tonight." Norah laughs.

"Got it boss." I didn't mind the extra champagne, I like my mimosa with just a hint of OJ.

Alana is pacing around the room with her hair half done and staring at her phone.

"Is she okay?" I whisper to Norah.

"I don't know. She's been on edge all morning." She frowns.

"I'll check on her." Wrenn says. "Excuse me." She tells the hairdresser.

Norah and I watch as Wrenn walks over to Alana and tries talking to her. We can't hear what she's saying but based on the facial expressions, it doesn't look like it's going well. Heather is back, but Gemma is in the bathroom getting dressed and Kim is putting on her necklace. Wrenn reaches for Alana but she snaps her arm back aggressively and storms out of the room. Wrenn sighs and retreats back to her seat next to me.

"What happened?" I whisper and Norah leans in to listen.

"I have no clue. All I asked was if she was okay. She started telling me all the things that went wrong and then she said she was going for a walk, alone." Wrenn explains.

"Maybe it's just wedding nerves, but I don't remember you like this." I look at Norah. I hate to bring up Finn today, but I didn't have anyone else to compare it to.

"Everyone's different, but no. On my wedding day I felt calm, like I was finally going to be with the love of my life." Norah smiles and places a hand on her belly. She barely had a bump yet, but she was already so attached to the baby.

"How long until the wedding?" Wrenn asks.

"About an hour. But it takes at least fifteen minutes to get her dress and veil on. Plus her hair isn't done." Norah says anxiously looking at her phone.

"Give her ten minutes then someone will go looking for her." I decide. It was best not to overpower her or add to her stress.

Gemma asks for some help zipping her dress, so Norah disappears to help her. When our hair and makeup is done, Wrenn and I head into the adjoining room to get dressed together.

"No funny business." I warn Wrenn.

"Yeah, yeah." She rolls her eyes.

"But maybe later? I was thinking about grabbing a hotel room for us."

Wrenn winces. "I don't know if you and I have the best history when it comes to weddings and hotel rooms."

"What if this was a way to rewrite our history?" I suggest.

"I'd like that." She softens with a smile.

"Good." I lean in to kiss her. Her lips soft with the same lipstick as me.

"You're gunna smudge it!" She complains.

I just laugh and slide out of my clothes, tossing them onto the bed for later. Wrenn looks me over, watching my body as I bend over to pick up my dress and let it slide over my head. She looks at me like something to eat and I groan.

"Just knowing you're going braless in that dress is going to kill me." She smirks as she slips behind me to zip the dress.

"You're going to have to work on keeping your hands to yourself today." I warn her. But I can feel her cool breath on my shoulders and all I want to do is let her take me on this bed.

"You guys dressed?" Norah knocks on the door and Wrenn and I jump apart.

"I am!"

"Gemma's going to look for Alana, okay?"

"Okay!" We call through the door.

"Why did that feel like my mom almost caught us?" Wrenn whispers.

I laugh and sit on the bed as she gets undressed. Wrenn places her clothes next to mine and grabs her dress off the hanger. She's wearing a thin white lace thong and no bra which is also going to drive me crazy. But I don't give her the satisfaction of telling her that.

"I love you." I say quietly. It falls out of my mouth before I can think about it and my eyes widen in terror as Wrenn turns around, her mouth agape.

"I love you too." She says after a moment. My face relaxes as she smiles and everything fades away.

"You do?"

"Yeah, I just didn't want to be the first to say it." Wrenn laughs.

"Oh my goodness! You are so freaking competitive."

"You really love me?" She wraps her arms around my waist and pulls me close.

"Yes. I do." I nod.

"Thank fuck." Wrenn's lips find mine in haste and she's no longer worried about her makeup.

I have to pull away from her before she ruins both of our hair and Alana kicks us out of the wedding. I zip up Wrenn's dress and we both walk back into the suite. Gemma's walking back in at the same moment.

"Uh, I don't know how to say this. But I can't find Alana." Gemma says quietly.

Acknowledgments

To Teddy, thank you for being my biggest supporter and telling me to "go write" when you want to play with your toys by yourself. And when you sit at my desk and type on my keyboard because you "want to be a writer like mama".

To my book author besties JJ Grice, M Leigh Morhaime, Tori Ellis, & K Leigh. Thank you for the overwhelming support and always being around for sprints or to talk about books or spicy scenes. Or to tell me I need to be writing when I'm not.

& lastly but not least, thank you to anyone who's picked up this book! Readers are what keep me going. I wouldn't be able to do this if it wasn't for you guys!

Check out Gemma and Norah's Story!

Check out Gemma and Norah's story in *To Be Loved!*
Preorder Now!

Also by Shannon O'Connor

SEASONS OF SEASIDE SERIES

(each book can be read as a standalone)

Only for the Summer

Only for Convenience

Only for the Holidays

Only to Save You

LIGHTHOUSE LOVERS

Tour of Love

Hate to Love You

To Be Loved

Inn Love

Love, Unexpected

ETERNAL PORT VALLEY SERIES

Unexpected Departure

Unexpected Days

STANDALONES

Electric Love

Butterflies in Paris

All's Fair in Love & Vegas

Fumbling into You

Doll Face

Poolside Love

Eras of Us

Tangled Up In You

THE HOLIDAYS WITH YOU

(each book can be read as a standalone)

I Saw Mommy Kissing the Nanny

Lucky to be Yours

The Only Reason

Ugly Sweater Christmas

POETRY

For Always

Holding on to Nothing

Say it Everyday

Midnights in a Mustang

Five More Minutes

When Lust Was Enough

Isolation

All of Me

Lost Moments

Cosmic

Goodbye Lovers

About the Author

Shannon O'Connor is a twenty something, bisexual, self published author of several poetry books and counting. She released her debut contemporary romance novel, *Electric Love* in 2021. O'Connor is continuously working on new poetry projects, book reviews, and more, while also diving into motherhood. When she's not reading or writing she can be found watching Disney movies with her son where they reside in New York. She is currently a full time mom and full time author.
She sometimes writes as S O'Connor for MF romances and as Shannon Renee for Poly romances.

Heat. Heart. & HEA's.

Check out more work & updates on:
Facebook Group: https://www.facebook.com/groups/shanssquad

Website: https://shanoconnor.com

facebook.com/AuthorShanOConnor
instagram.com/authorshannonoconnor
bookbub.com/authors/shannon-o-connor
pinterest.com/Shannonoconnor1498
threads.net/@authorshannonoconnor